AF225172

Blood Ore

Neal Andrew

Published by The Academy of I (org, 352670)

ISBN 978-1-9164087-5-3

Copyright © 2020 Neal Andrew

All rights reserved

Neal Andrew has asserted his rights under the Copyright, Designs and patents act, 1988 to be identified as the author of this work.

All rights reserved. This book or parts thereof may not be reproduced in any form, stored in any retrieval system, or transmitted in any form by any means - electronic, mechanical, photocopy, recording, or otherwise - without prior written permission of the publisher and author.

Acknowledgements

Cover photo – Ian Dooley

With many thanks to Cathy Stronach with whom
this adventure began.

I am also indebted to my editor, Tricia Johnson, without whom
this book would have remained silent.

Contents

Foreword

'The poetry of earth is never dead.'

John Keats

1995 St. Thomas's Parish, Jamaica

We were fast asleep that evening when the encampment shuddered and began to slip down the mountain. Red earth tore from rock, liquified then churned into cold night. The raging torrent rushed down and over the nearby cliffs, cutting a deep gulley before spilling its contents like an open artery into the Caribbean Sea. The black stain fanned out across the waves, carrying with it uprooted trees, smashed buildings, and tons of machinery. Only the oil drums bobbed aimlessly on the outgoing tide. For a little while our row of huts lay still, bloodied under the full moon showing silver through cloud.

In the aftermath, walking above the falls beyond the parish of St. Thomas, I could hardly bring myself to look at the devastation. The landslide had changed everything. Friends I'd held dear were gone. It was hard to believe there was no trace of the cabins we'd lived in all last summer. The grassy sunlit slopes and the huge Caterpillar excavators had all collapsed into the earth or tumbled from the bluff. Venturing up to the wide chasm, still unfenced and prone to landslips, I stood as close to the edge as I dared. Down among the tyres, planking, cables and tangles of fencing, I could see some muddy clothing and crushed DALCO helmets. On the bluff above a lone radio mast now leaned awkwardly from where our main office had stood; its wavering shadow surrounded by a thick slurry of mud and boulders shimmered in the light. The mine was silent now – its vapid air missing the characteristic smell of bauxite's 'pregnant liquor.'

The memories of our lives here echoed through the breeze. All our hopes and dreams which had seemed so real at the time were still so vivid and alive in me. It was hard to discard them, even now. We had made plans for everyone, plans to travel together – plans to live like there was no tomorrow. When I think of the others now, the grating sound of the once-busy chemical plant fills my ears again and I see the six of us together on the beach, in the hut or out walking along the bluff. But there is little use in dwelling on the past or in building regret for the things we either did do or did not do at the time. I took to the open again and looked back from the clifftops. In an odd way the sky looked different to me. Gazing west up over the bare rocky scarp, the heavens now sat uncomfortably on a jagged, saw-toothed ridge that wasn't there before.

Some say what happened at the mine was divine retribution, some think not. Others, when asked, pause for a moment then push by, happy to have avoided the conversation. But the fact is hardly any folks here say what they really feel at the best of times. On this island, where spiritual matters mix with arcane beliefs, the old traditions hold sway. To speak out is to break an unwritten code – to offend the governing spirits or *Loa*. Ask a local about the DALCO disaster and they will merely nod and say – nothing. You cannot ignore the certainty that the voodoo believers have their own way of dealing with death. The land here is still primal, even if the inhabitants seem less so. But this is their country. The ground they live on is their true mother. She suckles them and the loss of her blood grips their very souls. Many who follow the white-faced Obeah, who sings of mortal sin running hand in hand with science, live in terror of being struck by abnormal maladies. Processions of believers had already trailed across the remnants of our base, crossing and re-crossing the paths – throwing powders and splashing chicken blood. For here the just and the unjust demand redemption because sin, science and divinity bow before a cult power in Jamaica: superstition.

Whatever your belief, the red swathe we cut through the palms and green turf that year opened a scar on the mountain which marred the face God gave it. Seen from the bay, the ends of the cut sloped down in line with the rock beds, giving the ridge a wry smile — a smile that became a ghastly red grimace after the rains when it glistened wetly in the sun.

I come to the bluff now less and less. You may ask, 'Why do I still come at all?' I don't really know. All I know is that I survived, whilst many did not. I can't explain it further. All told, I'm a devout believer in nothing, but I was humbled by the powers of this earth when the mine vanished into darkness. It felt to me like half the mountain had suddenly floated up on wings, weightless, only to rush back into the belly of the earth or crash headlong into the sea.

Some nights I relive the disaster. Events play back in strobe-like flashes, often out of sequence; I hear chest-thumping remnants of sounds and stark images roll over me. I see stricken faces among flickering lights and hear again the screams pulling at the search beams. I lie awake at night as one scene plays over and over, with a curious switch from emotion to disassociation that makes me feel at times like I wasn't or shouldn't have been there at all.

The day before the slide, in cryptic warning, wildlife had scattered. Birds took to the air and dogs howled to be let loose. But no matter their howling, nor the constant whine of machinery, the rumble of the ore crushers, dozers or the blaring car horns, that day, like so many others, passed in scientific ignorance.

Science or God? Take your pick. You might, if you think on it long enough, see that on this island both are as real and unreal as any truth can be.

Chapter 1

A Girl in Limbo

Palisadoes Airport, Jamaica 1994

Leaving Jamaica from Kingston Town you drive out along Palisadoes, a long curving tombolo of sand lying off the bay. Heading south from the mainland, the sound of the city fades gently as the air freshens. Under blue skies, with a light headwind and the slow sound of the ocean in your ears, you turn towards the wide expanse of Kingston harbour, once a stunning turquoise cove, now a wasted, landlocked lagoon busy only with rusting dredgers and an endless flow of container ships. Palisadoes is all that remains of the old town after a tidal wave sunk the infamous Port Royal City in 1692.

It was late autumn, nearly two years before the slide and I was driving two DALCO men to the airport, Billy Thorne and Craig Sansano. Both were hard-bitten, tired men who'd seen too much, made too much and lost too much. It was hotter than usual on that late September afternoon and as we passed by the Maritime Institute, the sun was tilting its last rays across the rough concrete dolosse, those big, square concrete blocks that run the length of the open beach to protect the shifting sands. In the white glare I checked the wheel repeatedly as my big, overweight car fought pitted tarmac. The steady bumping had irritated Sansano and he began shouting in my ear.

"For Christ's sake, Clark, turn the fucking wheel! Avoid the buggers!"

In the rear view I saw he'd taken firm hold of the door but was still bouncing around like a rag doll. Thorne, bundled next to him, was curled up like a child, with a bulging briefcase firmly wedged between his knees. Even under duress I could hear the man still muttering about his bet slips and the three o'clock at Cayamanas Park. He'd already told me twice that a jockey he'd backed to ride three winners that day had been fined for 'intimidation and interference caused to scar.'

I turned off Palisadoes highway and onto the sand-blown Buccaneer Beach road. The turn was more for peace of mind than any direct aim for the airport. The road surface here was finer — a smooth rolled clay. I wound the windows down and looked out across the harbour. The sky touched the open sea in the distance and south east off the quay an untidy line of Palms blew lazily in the wind. Finally, I felt I had space to draw breath. A slow Cabral hopper dredger, sounding its horn, had just turned and was steaming doggedly toward the point now. At least on Buccaneer Road the going was quieter. Sansano had settled down a little and he was now rifling through his pockets for a cigar. To be frank, I'd had my fill of both these men and their macho posturing.

The last three weeks had seen us all cooped up in camp until their survey of the bluff had been completed. During this time, we were all confined to billets. My team had worked three double shifts just this last month, with all leave cancelled. And, like the men on Arawak ridge, they had complained bitterly about everything young men could complain about. In part, I could hardly blame them. The effort to survey the bluff — over three hundred acres of thick-soiled cliff-top — had hit us all hard. The overriding tension wasn't just due to us going stir-crazy either. Some of the rigging guys had told me the harnesses were well beyond their years and that it was more often stupidity which caused accidents — not mistakes. Mistakes could be forgiven, but not stupidity. I admit at that point I pitied Thorne when I heard he was told they would increase his danger money. When the pressure was on, DALCO were as bad as any other outfit for cutting corners.

The surveys across the bedding planes showed up several deep unconformities – which is geology speak for 'possibly dangerous' if you remove too much of the top layers. Below the overhang there were further traces of these fault lines. As bureaucracy goes, Dalmaine Mining Corporation (DALCO) was very similar to other Alumina refineries; they published only government-declared reports. All other documentation was kept secret. Whatever practice was rubber-stamped by Government House; DALCO bureaucracy continued in a come-what-may attitude. Several companies were working in the same district along with the same sub-contractors, like Jack Mulholland's Black River Transport and Mezon Freight Inc., a dubious quayside freight handler. The whole show was a mishmash of unconformity, not just the landscape. But in general, we persevered, replacing topsoil where necessary and replanting cleared trees, plus any rare or endangered flora that we'd removed before surface mining began.

DALCO had flown Sansano and Thorne in from Florida to monitor creep and to core the rock strata on the bluff. It shouldn't have been a particularly tough job. Across these hillsides, thick beds of virgin ore lay unmined. Cutter crews were due to open a new bauxite seam at the end of the month. Two or three days at most should have seen the fieldwork completed. But the site had proved more complex and now inspectors were on hand and they just weren't satisfied. Local officials had argued with Sansano's findings and told Thorne to remap the bluff. Thorne, who was primarily a core sampler, had plenty of experience, but he was not a good climber. DALCO knew his report would have to include a cross section of the overhang, and they pushed him hard to get it. To give him his due, Thorne kitted up and threw himself heartily into the task, but we could see he was far from happy. If the resulting strata were flawed and the bedding planes widened uphill, it could spell trouble when the topsoil was removed. Fissures would infill and then the planes could be forced apart.

I watched Bill Thorne clamber like a black ant across those cliffs for days. Saw him stretching out almost horizontal on the old harnesses, exploring the overhang, sixty meters in depth. Arawak ridge overlooked Morgan's Bay where the coastline whispered a breezy 500 feet below him.

The beach road was deserted now and the sea had turned a deep blue green. Cloud cover was moving in, already showing grey-white over the hills shrouding Kingston. I watched small details of the low houses disappear in the darkening light. I tried to shake off my thoughts and think about the beauty of this place. Changing gear, I stretched my shoulders and pulled the sun visor down. The engine rumbled on. The hypnotic drone of the tyres had smoothed now to a singular whine. My neck was still aching from the last few days of craning up across the bluff. I hoped this drowsy afternoon would whittle itself down to evening quickly. Then I could be rid of my acerbic cargo. As it turned out, there was no need for me to have worried; mother nature had other wonders in mind for me that afternoon.

We motored on past the weed-strewn dolosse that showed the extent of the high tide on this side of the bay. I checked the rear view again. The boys looked sleepy now. Had the murmur of the sea soothed the poor things? I noticed Thorne's eyes were following the passing lines of drought-stricken palms as they furled in the harbour-side breeze. He was waiting for a call trackside on his Motorola. The long avenue of palms had grown up along the old shoreline above the road. Now the slow dip and sway of their drooping branches caressed us in shade. It was time to for me to lighten up. The sun willed it – but my conscience fought it. Anyhow – whatever else happened this afternoon, I knew that before dark I would be driving back through the cooler mountain roads to St. Marys'. The drive home was always pleasant. I lived above Ocho Rios where my view of the sea was eternal. I had always preferred the North side of the island to Kingston and the Southern ports where industry and tourism fought bare knuckled for space. To my thinking home is not just where the heart is; home is where freedom is felt most. The Parish had proved lucky for me so far. Living outside the jungle of Kingston, with the mine just a few miles to the west of Ocho Rios, was both convenient and convivial.

Newcomers often think Jamaica an island Paradise – to some the tropical romantic coves and beautiful white sand beaches are simply that – but finding a living that pays you well down the years can prove tough. Admittedly the tourist does have the best of it, while the expats have to fight to survive. The summer months drag by wherever you live on the island and whatever you do. The slow tempo of crop picking amid the sloth of the townships, where life under tin roofs is unpleasant, remains wholly ingrained. There is little opportunity for blacks to leave the island. They need permits and passports to go to the States and most applications are disallowed. Summer here is either the artificial season of aircon and worsted suits faced in sterile offices, or the blazing heat and sudden storms of the outdoors. But why today of all days had cooled so slowly was still a mystery to me. I looked at the dash clock. We were very early, more than two hours before their flight. I wondered how on earth I was going to stand the wait. A private hire North-Star seaplane would land at the international airport in ninety minutes, if DALCO had kept to its schedule. With another glance back at Thorne and Sansano, I drove us into the old Victualling Yard and pulled up at Jacob's bar, a no-frills haunt popular among locals. You could hire a day-boat here, or just drink away the hours on dusty afternoons.

I had a fond affection for Jacob's that stretched back to my early days in Kingston. It was a clean, clinker-built place, dimly lit and smelled always of spiced rum and the potent smoke of Grabba tobacco. I jerked my head round as Sansano leapt out of the car before we came to a complete stop. "Jesus!" I yelled at him. Sansano took no notice. He was already half-way to the door by the time Thorne and I emerged into bright sunshine. I took a slow breath. I just had to force myself to keep calm for a couple more hours, then I'd see the back of these Florida hustlers.

I turned to look out to sea. Small waves lapped the sand near the Dolosse. I watched the rippled wake of yet another sleepy container ship roll up to the point. It felt good to stretch my legs as I angled myself against the old Chevy. I'd picked her up for a song from a kid who'd won it in a bet last year. He didn't say how. She badly needed a paint job, but the engine was sound and the aircon was in full working order. I shielded my eyes as I watched Thorne pull his suit into a suitable shape. After he'd finished smoothing himself down, he trailed after Sansano. The street ahead was deserted. Well, at least it was a beautiful day. So much so it seemed a shame to spoil my new-found liberty with a sour stint indoors. I dutifully followed the men inside the bar, which was not busy. Sansano was standing in the middle of the hall, gazing around among the brown tables. As I entered, he spun round on me, planting his hands down firmly on opposite chair backs.

"Well, here's the man! You sure know how to spring a treat, Clark. I give you that. Now, just how old is this mucky place?"
I shook my head and refused to answer. His grin, which bedeviled me at the best of times, leered animalistically. Thorne walked quietly up to the long zinc bar.
"Craig, as long as it's old enough to serve beer, I don't give a damn," he croaked. Sansano tossed his head back then watched me follow Thorne to the bar.

Saints and sinners could drink easy at Jacob's, when respectfully left to their own devices. And if you, like them, enjoyed talk of old Jamaica, then the waterfront captains and crewmen would take great delight in spiking your drinks with horrific tales of pirate slaughter, haunted plantations and lost Spanish treasure, most of which were surprisingly true. But you had to stay aware by degree, not to completely let yourself go, or else trouble would find you. Swirling among the smoke and harsh laughter, tidal hawkers would sometimes play a trick to try and catch you off-guard. They would toss an empty shot glass at you as you turned from the bar with your hands full of drinks. It was hard not to drop a full glass in order to make a reflex catch. The first time it happened to me I clapped two glasses hard together and got covered in beer and smashed glass. The silly pranks and colourful stories were followed by more colourful drinks and the night would often end in an invite to dive the bay at sunrise. But sometimes, things happened a little differently. On that hot, blustery day in October, I met the love of my life there.

Sansano and Thorne had pulled two stools up and were sat forward, leaning heavily on the bar top. Their well-tailored suits hid the fact they were out of shape. To locals, they looked like they earned big money - in comparison, that was most likely - but the whole truth told a different story. Thorne pulled his straw hat about, trying to reshape the crown. His fingers twitched with worry. The man was generally quieter than Sansano – but just as insistent, just as highly strung and irritable. In the canteen once, cutters had overheard him trying to pass the buck to Sansano. Thorne had hated it up on Arawak ridge and was determined to let the others know it, dragging Sansano's reputation down to his own red-faced grimace. I noticed his small eyes had a bad habit of darting past you when he talked, and he seemed always short of time.

Sansano played the richer, sassy, ladies' man about town. There was little about him of the academic engineer, but I think that varnish had worn off long ago. He talked a lot about money and about women too, but to me, both men lacked the bravado of true big shots. They complained bitterly if a certain comfort wasn't provided or if they had to endure insults from the crews.

I climbed onto a stool and sat alongside them. A local lad was watching us. I nodded my hello to him then turned back to Billy Thorne. Thorne, who deliberately ignored the lad, smirked at me, then pushed his hat back to a rakish angle. I ordered two whiskeys to start us off and a Red Stripe for me. Sansano sighed as he dabbed a soiled handkerchief over his blotched face.

"There's no air in here, Clark. And fuck me sideways! Look at the pinboard! A calendar from 1980?"

Sansano held up his drink for a moment. The glass was highly polished. He drank the shot down in one and seemed satisfied despite the look in his eyes.

"I don't remember 1980. Do you?" Thorne drawled.

"Hell no! And if I did, I don't want to go back."

Sansano shifted his gaze away from the faded Miss October 1980.

I knew that after working long shifts on the ridge, Thorne had gotten little sleep, having been doubled up in pain at night from the old harnesses which had cut into his groin. He was restless still, even now sitting with his legs spread wide for comfort. The ceiling fans had hardly touched the sweat rolling down his face. He'd been to the Doc before he left and the word was, he was in quite a mess. Meanwhile, Sansano had been out carousing with the *Sketels* in town. Sketel is patois slang for a promiscuous woman who preys on men — men like Thorne and Sansano. Now it's important, even with these men, not to think of it the other way around. The auction of sex in the Parish has been going on that way for centuries. The 'regular' prostitutes were camped near the mine. *Sketels* were simply flirtatious opportunists.

Sansano shouted to me, "Clark! Is the beer from 1980 too?"

I clucked my tongue at him. "It tastes like a vintage Mr S. But – I'd say more 1995."

Thorne laughed. "How precise. You're a master brewer now?"

Sansano turned away and pulled out his empty cigar case and twirled it in his brown hands. I looked at Thorne again. I knew he felt it had been worth all the pain and danger money he'd pocketed. Along with his support crew hauling equipment, safety ropes and even hammering the pitons in for him, he knew very well that Sansano should have been up there watching his back. Because of that, the pain in his groin and a dozen other grumbles, the man was still unhappy, placated only to a degree when he took a *sketel* last night. A foreman at the mine, Colt Brex, had told him there were plenty of house girls nearby, but precious contractors like Sansano and Thorne preferred shanty town women.

The young Negro sitting near me put down his empty shot glass with a sharp tap. I caught the notion but ignored it. I knew what he wanted. Instead, I ordered more whisky for Sansano and Thorne and another Red Stripe for me. Then I turned my attention to the lad. He looked me up and down, trying to second-guess my game perhaps. I saw he was red-eyed from smoking ganja.

"Stand *me* one, misser?" he said. Then pushing the empty glass toward me he smiled. I looked down at his hands. His knuckles were salt burned, the skin cracked white in the folds and sore. I saw he wore rough, makeshift boots made from leather flaps tied together with pink string. He looked at me steadily now with his red swollen eyes, pulling often at his jersey to unstick the dirty mustard material from his chest. He summed up perfectly the kind of jackals who plied a living here from bar to bar.

"Name's Clark," I said.

"Folks call me Hemp." I looked away and tried to hide my smile. Well, the lad was spry, edgy and no doubt out to make a fast buck!

"Well, *Hemp*, pleased to meet you," I said. "What's your poison?"

He smiled and chewed down hard on some Quaco leaf before answering me. I guessed he ate it to soothe his hands which looked very painful. "Appleton's," he said quietly. I motioned for the barman.

Outside, it was almost sunset now and the long yellow beams of sunlight that slipped through the gaps in the blinds striped the zinc bar. Eyeing the lad, Thorne pulled his briefcase closer to his stool. He was always careful with his papers Thorne, I'll give him him his due. In fact, today he seemed more than usually nervous about his briefcase. I began to wonder if he'd been paid in cash, or if there was something inside it of greater value to DALCO.

"Appleton's, Misser?" the lad said again, drily. The barman, a tall, hobbled Negro, Yellow Jack by name, came up slowly. He poured Hemp the last shot in the bottle. With all the delight of a child in his eyes, the lad watched his glass fill. When Jack was done, the lad snatched up the drink and downed it as if it might be stolen from his hand before his mouth got to it. I nodded to Yellow J.

"On me."

"Charity's a fine thing, Clark — if you wants *nuthin'* back." The waspish-tongued barman narrowed his eyes. It was just his way of keeping things straight between us.

Jack was as old as the furniture here. One afternoon, he told me that he was named after the bouts of 'Yellow Jack' fever he'd suffered as a kid. Thorne, observing the old barman kneel up on a stool to change an optic, pulled a disgusted face at the ugly scar which ran the full length of his right calf muscle.

"How d'you get tha-?" he began, but Yellow J. held up a hand before he turned to face him.

"Ah, seen ya lookin'," he said touchily. Then his mouth softened.

"Well fella, if ya gotta know, five years back my leg caught on a rusted stanchion off Lime Cay. Dat finished my diving career same day. Since then I bin here. Serving the coldest Red Stripe this side of de harbour."

Yellow Jack turned and idled back to a brown-stained sink where he rinsed his hands. He was touchy about his leg, and many had thought the injury had been the final straw that led to his wife and kid leaving him a few months later. The women here need a healthy, working man. The poverty line sits hard up against death, whichever way you look at it. Now, with his deep hoarse voice and big hands, Yellow J worked the bar, moving slowly but rhythmically about the place. I knew he earned barely enough to keep himself, but Jack seemed happy enough.

The lad eyed me warily. He'd swallowed his drink down in one.

"Thanks, Misser," he said, smacking his lips.

I could see he wanted another immediately, but I decided to make him wait for it. In the darkened beer hall, the line of fans above the bar stools struggled to keep us cool. Their dull hum thrummed in the sullen atmosphere. Sometimes a blade or two gave a squeak.

At this time of day the bar bathed us in an ochre twilight, drowning the rest of the spectrum in dark nicotine stains. The ceiling was covered in sheets of embossed leather, which hung loosely in circular patches. The dark wood blinds were clod-thick with dust. Yellow Jack barely ventured forward of the bar to tidy or to clean, but he habitually wiped the bright metal free from spills and smears. The surface of the bar gleamed like a newly minted coin. Perhaps he thought that wood cleaned itself? Suddenly the door banged open. A gang of traders from Hellshire beach came in. They huddled into a corner and started to argue fiercely over piles of green coconut. The hard bargaining brought a tall man to his feet. He threw down a pile of empty net bags and thudded his fists on the table. The thumping echoed his intention. Words flowed fast, spat in local Patois, most of which I didn't catch. The man wore a wide-brimmed fedora and a leather cross belt. I watched him unholster the long machete which he wore at his hip. He laid the blade crosswise on the net bags. Then he started to count out the coconuts. This sudden interruption had drawn all our heads. Sansano, who'd been watching indifferently, was first to turn his back on the argument. He shook his head then slid open his pigskin cigar case and tapped out two empty tubes. He twitched disappointedly, then stood the aluminum tubes on the bar. I turned to Hemp who looked forlorn as he stared at his upturned shot glass. It was hard to tell if he was mocking Sansano. But then the lad magically sprang to life.

"So! Who yo' friends?" he cried, smiling. "Y'all staying long?"

I smiled at his outburst. "Well! They are both leaving. I work in St. Katherine's. You?"

"Oh, ah gotta boat."

"I see. How's business?"

"Slow."

"Too bad. Got a missus?"

"No." the boy laughed. "Am too young for that foolery!"

"You fish?"

"D'pends – 'pends on what de fellas want."

"And what do you think I want?" I asked him playfully.

"C'mon, Huck," he said, beckoning me.

"Clark," I corrected him, staying put.

"Clark, den. We can take my boat now if yo wants. Yo got plenny time. Dive Port Royal. Not so deep." His sing-song words caressed his pitch.

"I'm sure licenses are involved, aren't they?" I said. "Have you got one?"

I slid a few dollars to the barman as Yellow J hovered. He smiled as I nodded at Hemp's empty glass. "Would you like another?"

"Sure!"

Jack grabbed a stool and took down a new bottle from the show bar, held the label up close to his eyes then shook his head as Hemp continued the hard sell.

"Diving's good! Water — clear as glass."

"And on a sunken city too . . . How much, may I ask?"

"Oh, we get to that, Misser! Price d'pends"

"Meaning on what we haul? Is it protected?"

"Plenny folks find gold coin there," Hemp blinked slowly then continued excitedly. "Needs juss an hour or two." I nodded back to Jack and he uncorked the bottle. Hemp drew some stained papers from his pocket and a few strands of leaf. He began to lay down a paper and arrange some slivers of tobacco. A dirty one-dollar note fell onto the bar from his sleeve. I watched him unroll it. Unrolled, it looked like no dollar note I'd ever seen.

Sansano was sitting drawing 'finger music' from the rim of his glass, bemused by all the patter, and content only to comment by gratuitously puffing on his last cigar. The great blue-grey clouds added to the stifling atmosphere. I could feel my eyes stinging. I looked back at Thorne, at the hunched shoulders and the way he'd pulled the brim of his soft hat down. He was still flicking through the same dozen or so pink bet slips, equally irritated by the loud argument nearby. I watched him ease his neck about his collar line, in a kind of habitual reflex – as if he needed to grease the gears of his neck from time to time. Sansano moved the cigar to the other side of his mouth. He whispered something to Thorne and in turn both men nodded almost mperceptibly. Thorned tapped his briefcase gently. The arguent had grown fiercer now. I knew what was coming.

"Jesus, Clark!" Sansano erupted. "This place is a sodden relic, ain't it? Poor Thorne here can't cash his bets! And you've buried us alive in a den which never sees the light of day! Now it's raining profanity! And take it from me — there's no reason to encourage this darned lad any further."

"Yeah, another day, fella," rasped Thorne, who'd caught the tail end of the objections between mentally totting up his losses. Sansano leaned in front of Thorne and whispered to me. "Your little bitta fun is going to end badly. Believe me, friend. And that's not all."

I looked away from the slitted eyes pressing his meaning. Between drink, women, money and the severe itch to escape Jamaica, the man was so full of shit. Hemp, who may have overheard us, gave me a puzzled look.

"Have another?" I offered, looking at him kindly. Sansano zipped his pigskin case up and felt for his wallet. Yellow Jack, with a look of contempt at both my colleagues, poured more glasses of Appleton's for us.

"On de house fellas!"

Hemp gave us both a big grin; the sort of mile-wide toothy grin you'd associate with a sudden reversal of fortune. I toasted him and Yellow J. and offered another round to Sansano and Thorne. Then I wondered how long I could play this charade. I still had to drive back to St Mary's and then over to DALCO's head office in Ocho Rios later this evening. Maybe Sansano was right. Maybe I should quit the farce while I was ahead.

"Tell me about the dive business Hemp. Do you maintain your own gear? You use Oxy 80s, yes? Steel or alloy cylinders?" The lad suddenly looked disconcerted.

"Scuba needs a two-man crew, doesn't it?" I continued, smiling at Sansano.

"Who's your partner? Have you got signal flags, radio, a compressor?" In response, Hemp felt under his armpits again and sniffed both his hands.

"Look, ah was fishin' early dis mornin'. I juss go clean up, Misser. Then we git goin'— if yo still got time." He put his empty on the unrolled dollar. Then he took off suddenly. Sansano laughed and leaned back from his stool.

"Did you see his pink laces beat him to the door? You sure got him excited, Clark."

Thorne lifted his head. Two throbbing veins stood out on his forehead.

"Why do you do that, Clark? Why get him so hot? Now he means to buzz the wharf, find some scuba gear, fuel, a mate and take us all for a tidy sum. You darn near gave him a full itinerary!"

Craig poked his tongue out, tasting the air. His sarcastic tone chimed. "Well, let's see now – be an hour for three of us? Say — fifty dollars plus air, suits and fins? Maybe a hundred bucks all in? A hundred bucks to drown in some broken-down tub – or suffocate on a bad mix. Is that a satisfying afternoon or what?"

"Count me out," I said.

"Whaddaya think, Bill?"

"Well, right now I think at least the boy's not afraid of hard work."

Sansano paused, digesting the change in attack, then he slowly smoothed his thick, dark hair back with both hands. "What's that supposed to mean, bud? You still mouthing off about my nights in town? Still riled about me leaving you on the ridge?"

"Maybe!" Thorne growled. "Maybe I got a right to be sore."

"I did my share, Billy!" Sansano blurted angrily. He looked me in the eye again.

"You know, it'll take danger money to put a full crew up there, Clark."

"Not our worry, Craig," said Thorne quickly, turning his back to me and laying a hand on Sansano's arm. But the mere mention of danger money had got my full attention. It was my crew on shift next. DALCO were well known for cost-cutting, working men hard and ducking danger pay whenever they could.

"What's the worry?" I asked. "Something I should know? You've been nurse-maiding that briefcase all day. Got a report in there Thorne? Something I should see?"

Sansano looked away. Thorne was about to say something but changed his mind. He straightened up, opened his collar and unfolded his sunglasses from his top pocket. Sansano contritely wiped the head from his beer. The atmosphere buckled as froth pooled white on the zinc counter. But their nonchalance continued unabated. The subject was closed, scuttled for good. Thorne called Yellow Jack over.

"Got a radio, bud? I've a hot tip on the three o'clock at Cayamanas."

Jack shook his head, "Aerial broke a whiles. Sorry boss. But I got a phone. There's one outback if yo wants?"

Thorne clenched his fists in frustration.
"Nope. The phones are jammed solid. Every bookie worth a damn is on the rails takin' bets."

To settle the point, he shook his new Motorola in Yellow Jack's face. "Where's the radio?"

"Oh no matters. Can't be fixed."

"Why not?"

"Just can't …"

"Or won't? Jesus! You people make me sick." Thorne mopped his forehead.

"I got a dozen big bets on and nobody here gives a damn."

Bill Thorne was clearly a man whose bets swooped on anything that had the smell of success, like carrion-hungry birds. Sansano jostled his beer to and fro in front of him.

"So, where's the party today, Clark?" I knew immediately he was trying to provoke me.

"Still no boat, no radio, no women, and no bets! Seems an awful big waste if you ask me."

Sansano could be a dozen different men in an hour. You never knew which might appear next. The cynic, the hard-bitten wannabe millionaire or the joker. I shook my head as Thorne unfolded his biggest stake slip and looked mournfully at it.

"If it's a win, Billy, I'll collect it for you," I offered. I wanted to ask him about the ridge. Maybe he had a copy of the report with him. Lowly site crews were never party to any documentation. But how and when? I felt I owed my crew that much. I took a punt.

"Thorne . . . If there's anything I should know – about the ridge — just say it." Neither man replied.

At the end of the bar was a half-finished drink. It had been sitting there dead since we'd arrived.

"Gonna clear that, Jack?" I said, joining the downbeat mood of the others.

Sansano jumped in. "This place needs a buy-out, Clark. There's no fuckin' standards! Nuthin' clean, no parties, no nuthin'."

I watched the loud-mouthed ape draw shapes in his spilled beer froth with a matchstick, while drinking erratically from his glass as if he was being forced to swallow unpalatable things.

Thorne muttered aloud. "I bet that kid comes back with some phoney pieces of eight next, just to get us out in that stinking bay."

Yellow Jack came along cheerily, wiping down the zinc with a big chamois cloth.

"We got nice cold beer here, fellas. Ain't no need for a dive today. Enjoy your beers while they plenny cold."

He opened the bar flap and idled over to the traders at the back who were quiet now. He begged a fresh coconut, came back and put out slices along the bar on aluminum plates. I sipped my beer as Jack pulled a clean glass from the rinsing tap and polished it in front of me.

"How's things, Clark? Don't see yo so much these days."

"I'm a taxi man for DALCO now." I grinned. I saw Sansano grin too. Jack nodded slowly.

"Guess things are pretty good den. They say life depends on de company ya keep. Yo sure look happy."

I ignored the jibe. "I've got good friends in camp," I said cheerily. He looked at me blankly. "Sure — it's a noisy red devil of a life, Clark. But in here, don't I just serve the nicest cold beer!"

I sighed hard. Even with the fans turning the air, it was sticky and hot. I opened my shirt to the waist and helped myself to the fresh coconut. It was the sweetest thing I'd tasted all day. The white flesh was at least whiter than my sweat-stained T-shirt. I juggled the facts again. Thorne and Sansano were at best hard to please, but what more could I have done? All week, the atmosphere around them had been oppressive. Jack was watching both men carefully now as he wiped the bar again. I looked at my watch; forty minutes had just about trickled by. Funny how every minute sometimes registers the pain of each second contained within in it – like those Russian egg dolls, which sit one inside another, each trouble getting smaller and smaller but each a vitriolic, condensed version of the last until, finally, you were left with the most potent cluster of troubles you'd ever known in your life. Unpacked, they had you surrounded. For me, whatever was bright and big and beautiful often contained a thousand ills and whatever was simple and forthright and clean had always been besmirched in some way. These men knew something bad about the bluff that we didn't. I was certain of it. Then wham! Sansano slammed his palm down on an insect.

"Funny little beggars those are. Make you itch for days." The noise had destroyed what reverie I'd managed to find alongside these two and a beer, but the cold trade winds would blow in soon. November would turn over in grey shrouds and these men would be gone, long gone, and maybe if the good Lord was looking out for me and my crew, DALCO would find better pickings away from the bluff. Out of my daze, I wondered what to do. It was still an hour before check-in. This *was* my local of sorts, before I'd got the job at the mine.

"It's over-priced, *nice* cold beer," groaned Thorne belatedly.

"Have some coconut, Billy?" I offered, shoving a plate along.

"If I eat that, I'll be sick," he hissed.

"Sick is okay for those who wallow in it," murmured Sansano. The comment had bitten him as bad as the insects.

"What, like those town girls you got us last night?" Thorne snapped.

"They wallow in sundries, man. You see them? Even the main course is sundries, and if you don't oblige them with dollars – then out pours a bawlin' and a hollerin' to be heard three blocks away at three am by all and sundry."

Sansano smiled; "Yeah, sundry types are funny dames." He put his hands behind his head and leaned back. "I knew a sundry once; tall, black-haired, cute. She spoke through her nose and charged me through mine. Real nice gal, by all accounts – for a sundry."

Thorne continued the usual patter while mopping his neck. "Some woman ain't nothing but sundries," he said bitterly, leering at the bikini-clad calendar girl. Craig laughed and patted him on the shoulder.

"You cantankerous ol' bastard. You haven't changed a bit, Billy. C'mon. Let's put DALCO behind us. Let's put the whole damned week behind us. We got richer pickings to come. What do you say?"

Thorne shook his head, swallowed some beer and shrugged. Sansano looked back at me with his dark-circled eyes.

"Like the sound of that bullshit, Clark? See, we're having fun now, boy. Fun, fun, fun!"

Like hell, I thought, but I smiled at him to show goodwill. I began to feel some of their irritation was my fault for not taking them straight to the air-cooled lounges.

"Look, I thought you *boys* would hate airport bars — full of pickpockets, loose women and cramped for space."

"Loose women, eh?" Sansano whispered. "We should be so lucky. I never took you for a boy who enjoys a local *flavour* Clark. Thought you just came in here for coconut and smiles."

I swore at him, took out my wallet and counted out ten dollars. Thorne, at the prospect of leaving, brightened. "Man, you should have joined us last night, Clark!" he whistled.

"Those girls and them sundries!" He whistled again and finished off his drink. Sansano had at last managed to smooth things over a little between them.

"Look, Billy; the turf accountant got a booth at the airport. Why not collect your roll from there?"

Thorne sat considering the idea for a moment then looked at his watch. I pushed my empty glass towards Jack and waited. Craig tilted his head to one side, popping the vertebrae in his neck as he stretched his jaw wide open. He looked up at Jack, "If that drink is not cleared, then there must be somebody here we ain't met. She worth meeting?"

Jack came, lowered his head and whispered in my ear, "Clark, that a good customer. She not finished here. I don't want no trouble now. Yo settle your friends down quiet, ya hear, if she come out?"

"Yes, I hear. Nothing's going to happen."

I watched the Hellshire beach traders pack up their catch now. The tall Negro with the burly fists was first to pull his net bag closed. It was full to bursting with green coconut. Later he would walk the shallows along the Crown Line and sell them cut for drinking to beach-goers. I watched him sling the heavy bag across his muscled shoulders and start towards the door. The machete swung low from his hip. Along Montego Bay the tide hawkers traded with the old boatmen who brought them palm fruits and coca from nearby deserted islands. It was a quasi-symbiotic relationship which had its up and downs like any other. But some nights a beach hawker was found face down on the incoming tide.

A tall, flame-haired girl emerged from the washrooms. She turned her back on us as she walked to her stool at the far end of the bar. I watched her keenly. She had nicely curved hips and was dressed in pressed clean clothes. Her long red hair brushed her shoulders as she moved. She settled down and then began to check her things meticulously. She was unlike the type that dress to intentionally drag a man to his doom. This girl was no siren. She seemed to me to be perfectly beautiful, yet imperfectly aware of her sexuality. I watched her open a gold compact, part her lips, then roll them over each other, keeping her eyes level in the mirror. Then she tilted her head, this way and that and when satisfied, she slowly smoothed her eyebrows one at a time with her index finger. I watched the wide lips purse now and noted the poise of her long, sensual neck. I was enjoying her very much, studying the way she'd gathered her hair and unthinkingly pulled it over one shoulder. She seemed completely oblivious to my watching her and that was OK by me. Her movements were both delicate and elegant. Her ritual was a well-practiced one. Then she suddenly snapped her compact shut and broke my reverie. Sansano scraped his chin stubble with his thumbnail as he continued to eye her. Yellow Jack leaned over and whispered hoarsely.

"Now fellas – like I said, no use getting interested. Red got a man. He comin' in on Pan-American; four thirty. Name's Granby. Paul Granby. Rich fella."

Jack's voice crackled on under the swoosh of the fans like a transistor radio. All I could hear now was white noise; a blood rush from the girl, coupled suddenly with a dozen or so voices in my head, one asking her name and where she was from and the others – well, more puerile questions. I heard Jack whisper again and pushed a couple of dollars at him. I took more coconut and chewed on it slowly. The white flesh shone in the half-light. The barman kept a steady eye on me, then moved to block my view of the girl.

"Alright, Jack." I said quietly.

The room was quieter now but the initial rush I'd felt had not calmed. Sipping my beer, I glanced up at her now and again. She'd twice ordered a Black Russian and now Jack was trying to pour the Kahlua to her liking. She sipped at it between erratically going through her bag and looking up at the clock. I saw her become irate as the minutes ticked by. I forgot about Sansano and Thorne, the whole place misted over and sat paused in my peripheral vision, as if someone had stopped time with a stopwatch while just she and I went on living. Drunk and blinkered on sex and romance, suddenly I began to wonder if I truly realised just how much I needed a girlfriend.

Her fingers combed through a pocket of loose change inside her bag. She dug deeper and sighed louder. What had she lost? Then she tipped the entire contents of her handbag onto the bar. The clatter was followed by her long fingers picking through keys, tissues, lipsticks and a small sequined purse. Some coins rolled to the floor, but nobody bothered to pick them up. Was she really meeting Mr. Rich, I wondered? I homed in on her clothes. She was dressed primly in a navy-blue skirt and a crisp white blouse of embroidered cotton. Anyone could see she had tried hard to impress – too hard, maybe? Was she a worrier, a neurotic even? What was I letting myself in for? Looks are not everything – I heard those words in the voice of my father. Was that a point I'd learned? In fact, what had I learned about women in twenty-four years? I admit it was not much. Want was all I really knew. Just a deafening, searing want. Keats had taught me something of love and beauty and the wisdom of falling – of trusting my heart, of taking flight and of simply letting go whenever I saw true beauty. But in the cold light of day, all that felt wrong somehow – too sycophantic even. If it was true, it was a truth hard to swallow. All beauty creates is want, I thought. Take it or leave it. There was an entire philosophy in that. And right now, I wanted her. I wanted her like nothing else on earth. But first, I had to consider and settle on the fact that this Granby guy must matter to her in a big way.

A Hellshire trader came to the bar and asked for a rum double. His machete clipped the stool as he leaned in. Jack poured. He drank it, grabbed the bottle and two clean glasses and slowly went over to the girl. She paid him no attention until he pushed a glass and the bottle toward her.

"No thanks," she said quietly. I began to bristle and was getting ready to move when Yellow Jack cut in.

"Sit down, Jonty! Gal gotta fella coming in – big shot. She don' want no company."

The hawker spoke rapidly.

"I juss playin' wid her, Jacob. Red here look like she burning up. Thought I'd play wid sum fire. A fire needs company."

Another trader stood up and jammed the point of his blade hard into the table. Jonty looked over his shoulder, pulled a wry face and strolled back to his seat with the bottle of rum tucked under his arm. Yellow Jack sauntered over to me.

"Thanks," I said. "Know her name?"

"I call her Red but on the phone they called her Chase."

I had to smile — any man would. Sansano sliced into our conversation.

"When you boys finished ya hissy chit-chatting, I'll take three Robusto five-five Os Jack. I'm clean out."

He briefly showed his belly wallet full of new 50-dollar bills.

"That's forty-two bucks fifty," Jack said, slamming his palm on the bar. Sansano's squat, thickly veined hand passed him a note. Yellow J. pulled open a drawer, took out the metal tubes, counted them slowly, drew one delicately under his nose then gave Sansano the three fifty-ring Havana Grabba Leaf cigars.

Thorne had done with his beer now and was trudging to the door. He signalled me with a hand in the air "Clark, let's hit the road. I'm famished. You ready, Craig?" As he opened the door, Hemp fell in through it.

"Jeez! Yo boys leavin'?"

"Back off, pal!" Thorne spat, brushing past Hemp and dragging his briefcase clumsily through the gap between them. Sansano straightened his shoulders and refused the high five the lad offered him.

"Mebbe I see you boys later?"

I followed Sansano and wandered out into the sunshine. I glanced back at Chase, trying to catch her eye. Time was against me now. I hadn't said a word to her. Finally, my mouth got the better of my reserve. I stepped back inside and held the door ajar. You could feel the heat blowing in from the open door.

"Excuse me. But can I help? Have you lost something?" She eyed me up and down.

"No. My friend's plane's coming in. He's meeting me here later."

I looked into her eyes and tried to reassure her. I couldn't think of much else to say — at least nothing that would rock her world, nothing clever enough that might change her mind to thinking about me instead of this Granby. But perhaps that sort of switch only happened in movies. I did see tiredness and worry in the heavy lidded but graceful eyes though.

I hesitated for a moment longer, then introduced myself. "Clark Mason, DALCO Mining, up at St. Katherine's." I held out my hand. She ignored it, met my eyes briefly, trying to discern what I wanted. Her voice was softer, pleasant even, unless I imagined it. A black SUV suddenly drew up. I could hear voices coming from the street. Craig banged on the open front door.

"Clark! Shaw's here. He's gonna run us up to the airport. Let me have the keys, will you? I want to transfer the luggage."

I got up and threw him the keys to my Chevy. He caught them awkwardly whilst relighting his cigar. Thorne shouted back to me. "Clark! That DALCO camp."

"What of it?"

"It's a powder keg. One night the townies are gonna turn up, torches in hand – just like in Frankenstein. They'll burn the place to the ground. They got some big beefs with you guys. Believe me, maybe it's the start of a new Accompong war?"

He laughed at that, then his face became deadly serious.

"Forget the ridge – look further up, across the bluff . . . read the report. Don't say I didn't warn you. He handed me a small, carbon copy. The thin piece of paper was brittle. I crumpled it in my hand and tucked it into my pocket."

As Thorne walked away, Sansano turned and gave me that big fake smile of his again. He chewed the cigar to the side of his mouth and opened the boot of my car.

"Close the damn door!" Jack yelled. "Hemp! You comin' or goin? Make up your damn mind!"

Hemp slipped quickly back inside, and I slammed the door shut behind him. I thought of the girl then the report. There would be time enough later to read this report and see what the hell he was being so secretive about. I eased myself onto a bar stool nearer the girl.

"Hello, Chase." She didn't reply. "I know you're pie-eyed." I said, lighting up a cigarette.

She looked nonchalantly at me for a few seconds.

"Pie-eyed? Well, if I'm pie-eyed, then you're goggle-eyed Mister. You've been sitting there goggle-eyed all afternoon!"

I opened my mouth, but she beat me to it.

"Haven't you got somewhere else to be?"

Her voice was husky, soft — tender even. It fascinated me. I'd been warned off her but the dogged streak I got from my mother had flared up. I reached for the plate of coconut again.

"Well, today my somewhere else is here." I said. "In fact, I work on the other side of the island."

"Brave boy!"

"Thanks."

"It wasn't a compliment."

"Thanks again! But why lie to me?" I said, munching slowly.

"Sorry? Why what?"

"Why lie to me. I mean you are tight, aren't you? In plain sight and all that?"

I pushed the plate of coconut between us and took another piece.

"You want a lady to admit she's drunk — is that it?"

Smiling, I paused a few seconds and looked into her eyes. "Depends. Look, I only want to help. Can you walk? I'm serious."

"Sure, I can walk." She looked at me angrily now, mumbling something into her sleeve that sounded like, 'The freak type.' Her arm slid across the bar and she swept all her things back into her handbag in one motion. They tumbled into an assorted mess. I sucked down hard on the coconut flesh and wiped my lips on my arm. She pushed a stone ashtray towards me and called Jack over.

"Red Stripe, Jack. And ask this guy to move along. I can't stand bad company. You know how Paul gets. If he comes in, there might be trouble. He might break both his arms."

Jack smiled briefly, "I don't see nothin' wrong this time, Chase."

"Him being here is all wrong. And it's *Case*, not Chase."

I looked at her getting mad, flushing red in the heat of the moment. The fans above were whirring and wobbling in a feeble effort to cool us off. One at our end squeaked as it spun slower than the rest.

"Don't worry, Jack," I said. "She's sore at all mankind today."

"Am I?"

Yellow Jack shrugged. "I don't care. I'm not a damn chaperone. Just keepin' the peace, thass all"

"I don't care either," Case said, shoving her empty glass away. "Forget the beer, Jack. Keep it. God, sometimes men are such bastards!"

Jack idled away. I wondered if the outburst was aimed at me, but perhaps someone *had* ruined her day — or her life, even. Maybe today she had lost a shot at true happiness.

"When I say walk, Case, I meant home."

'Look, where do you get off talking to me like that? I don't need a slow reveal of my condition, of the … here and now … or anything I can't see or feel per… perfectly for myself. I've already told you more than I ought."

"Sorry," I said softly, "I never intended to offend." I noticed she'd stammered a couple of times through the last rebuke.

"Intentions? Well, that's what's wrong – isn't it?" She said into the air. "Funny how people always seem the have the *best* of intentions."

Her sarcasm hung heavy. She'd spoken with a drunk's over-emphasis. I swallowed my pride a little – maybe I *was* being too harsh. Another voice inside me chided that shrinking violets were not her type. Just be strong, be bold — but be fair, I told myself. I thought about buying her a coffee.

"Like I said, I'm here to help."

Case drew a long breath. "Do your friends always get into strange cars and leave you behind? If so, you must end up in the most godforsaken places."

I looked at her for a second.

"Oh, there are lots of places without god – but like most disbelievers, I still keep him right in here, see." I pointed to my heart. "Can't you see him? He's the poor sod who picks up waifs and strays every day of the week."

"I'm no … regular stray." She eyed me suspiciously.

"You think it's a foolish trait."

"I've known fools all my life."

"Did they get anywhere?"

"Depends on what fools they were."

"Just the common or garden fool will do."

"I like my fools on the wilder side."

"Maybe that's what's got you into this mess. Hiding out here, waiting for a plane that's never coming — least *not* with a particular passenger."

She looked shocked at that. I retreated from the comment. She pulled herself up to assume some kind of faux formality.

"So, now you think I'm a fool, do you?" she flared.

"I never said that."

"It's what you meant. Well, maybe I am. Maybe we are all just fools cheating at life."

"Who's cheating? I never said …"

She cut me off. "Don't say any more. I think we've both been foolish enough for one day, don't you?"

"Alright." Maybe it was time to say nothing, but something urged me on.

"You know nothing much about me yet — except that I like you. I just want a chance to help."

I watched her inwardly digest that. There *was* a hint of contrition in there somewhere. But I knew it would take more than a few wisecracks to sabotage the love of her life. I took a long draw on my cigarette. Between smoking and eating coconut, I took the time to think; time to gauge my progress. Underneath all the barracking she created a kind of space around us, a place I felt comfortable in. I looked closely into her eyes again. They were chatoyant, changing in the varied light, like fitful angry gemstones or a tiger's eye. I stubbed out my Craven A and exhaled.

"Look, if we've got off on the wrong foot, let me buy you a coff—"

"I don't care what foot, hand or brain we got off on. I thought we'd agreed – oh, persist and I *will* talk and you *won't* like it!"

"I see."

What to do? Suddenly I thought capitulation might work better than any chauvinistic attempt at supremacy. Maybe she'd let me in if I played submissive — at times, even shrinking violets have a place in the world.

"Okay, I give up. You win, sister." I stood up from the bar. "Can't say a man never tried."

She took a sip of her drink and looked straight ahead. I guessed if she didn't bite now that was it. Mr. *delightful* Granby was still coming for her. He could arrive at any minute. Then where would I be? Jack came along and I opened my wallet. I spoke in low voice.

"There sits a fire cat, Jack, and fire cats are fine, except when they're on fire and that fire is aimed at you. Boy, is she on fire now!"

They both looked at me, bemused. I grabbed my jacket.

"You goin' for help?" she said quietly, looking intently at her half-finished drink.

"Need a fireman?" She turned towards me.

"It's an ice man you need today, ma'am, and perhaps he will cometh!"

She smiled meekly. And there it was: that something about her, that something hard to place exactly; the looks, the lithe figure, the long, flaming-red hair, the devil-may-care attitude and the dozen or so other hard-to-put-your-finger-on quirks and habits she had. But, however idiotic, however struck by lightning it all seemed, I *was* hooked.

"I'm going cross-island. You need a lift?" I threw down my unfinished slice of coconut like a sodden gauntlet, lingered by her for a few moments before leaving two dollars on the bar. She said nothing.

On my way out I noticed a slip of folded paper caught in the door jamb. I picked it up. It was a note from a phone pad. Unfolding it, I read: *'Sorry, delayed. Won't be this week. Nor next. Della knows. I can't say more. Keep in touch, love Paul.'*

So, there it was, she'd known all along that he'd thrown her over. Case, a little now, saw the blue paper in my hand. I went back to her.

"Looking for this?"

"I guess you read it?"

"Yes."

"He's a shit!"

"A fool," I said.

"Don't lie to me," she whispered. I smiled back. Maybe I was standing in the firebreak now.

"Alright," I said. "He's a shit. A married shit?"

"What do you care?"

"I don't, but I'd like to apologise. For being pushy earlier."

"Just earlier?"

"Look, I said I'm sorry. We've both had a day of it. But I was right, wasn't I? It's a long walk back to Kingston. Now, if you're all done, Ma'am?"

I handed the note back to her. She screwed it up tight and dropped it into her bag. Then, scrunching her hair up, she put her head forward into her hands. I recognized that tired and blunted feeling. I felt the look, the exhaustion. I put another two dollars down under her glass.

"Allow me?" I said, taking her arm. "Keep the change, Jack." I turned to leave.

She stood up. "There's no need," she said. I let go of her arm.

Jack called out, "How do you know she not drinking champagne, Clark?"

"In here?" I exclaimed. "And if she was, it's only worth a five."

I grinned. He waved me out and to my surprise, Case got off her barstool and stood beside me.

"To hell with ya both, then," Jack said. Case followed me out to the car. Craig had left the keys under the rear tyre. We put our sunglasses on simultaneously and climbed in. I smiled to myself because I liked synchronicity — any and all synchronicity. In fact, I thrive on coincidence. I started the engine and turned on the aircon. Case tucked her bag into the footwell and made herself comfortable.

"We *were* going to a lovely hotel up the coast," she shouted over the motor. "Paul told me it would be a perfect weekend; with a perfect beach, perfect music, food and sunsets. What a fool I am."

"Where am *I* taking you?" I said.

"The Bristol."

"Harbour Views, isn't it?"

"Balfour."

"OK. Balfour on Sunset it is."

I pulled away and notched up the aircon. Her hair moved in the cooling stream of air. She shook her head slowly from side to side, basking in the breeze. The road would be clear now until we hit the fork. I let her alone a while as she closed her eyes and breathed in the evening sunshine.

After a few minutes she lifted her sunglasses.

"Mind if I ask something?"

"Shoot!"

"Are you always so persistent?"

"Maybe. Do you always give in so easily?"

She grinned a little. "Depends," she said, settling her sunglasses into her hair.

"If you knew Granby wasn't coming, why did you go to the bar?"

"Paul had phoned my hotel, but just missed me. I'd left early. We'd planned to meet at Jacob's anyway to avoid the crowds. Yellow Jack handed me the message when I arrived. I was in shock at first. But then after a few minutes it sank in properly and

I got angry and drank anything he threw my way. I tossed the jotting around; look, there goes my life – reduced to scribble!"

"Okay, so Paul just missed you leaving. But he could have spoken to you at the bar, explained in person. Cold-hearted fool, isn't he?"

"The worst."

"I know a perfect cure for betrayal."

"What?"

"Four cocktails, three times a day, and a new hat."

She looked away from my bad joke. I knew it was a stupid thing to say, but I still said it. Why did I always kid myself I could reform – I mean, in the face of true love? Really her life was no laughing matter.

"C'mon Case, have a drink, buy a new hat and look on the bright side."

She looked needled. I continued briskly. "You have a clear weekend now. A clearer life, perhaps?"

I drove across the fork and we took the main road into Kingston. The traffic was heavier now and we got snagged in a queue. We sat there silent for a few minutes, the engine thrumming, the light cutting through the smoked sun visor on the windscreen – two alone among the Palisadoes. She pulled her skirt tight to her knees and straightened her blouse.

"I have a cure for betrayal too," she said. "It involves balls. The loss of."

I glanced at her but said nothing.

"I didn't like your friends much, by the way. Who were they?"

"Not my friends. Surveyors from the mine."

"Well, like I said, I didn't like them." She stifled a shudder and breathed deeply.

"Are the locals really at the gates? I heard what the oily one said."

"No, the locals are just bellowing for work."

"I see." She seemed satisfied with that and lay back in the seat. I relaxed a little now. We were together and talking and the sky was a picture of darkening blue swirled in a gaudy cocktail of burnt vermillion.

"You lived here long, Clark?"

"Not long. Three months in Kingston. A year at DALCO. You?"

"A month or so. I'm not working. I was waiting on – well, never mind now."

"You have choices and this place has promise."

"I'm sick of empty promises! Maybe, I should just go up into the blue mountains and jump off somewhere."

I looked aside, catching her retreat into a sullen gaze. I changed down and got us moving again. Granby had a lot to answer for. I wondered what excuses he'd told his wife to explain his caper. Then I thought, to hell with it, maybe she knew all along.

The sun had dropped to the horizon in big fiery ball of red. Now it was the sweet-spot hour when the island basked in the more expensive sky-born liqueurs that faded from orangey Cointreau to purplish moonshine. The long shadows of the roadside palms swept across our faces as I drove us to Sugar Loaf Bay.

"After a month, Case, you learn to dodge the outside world a little. Those blue mountains are very beautiful day or night — cooler, high and with clean, dry airs."

"Sounds like a paradise for suicides," she said. I laughed at that, but she barely grinned.

"You can at least dodge the dollar traders there. But beware the storytellers. Here, under life's easy veneer, the old settlement roots go deep. They call Jamaica the rock. The people are 95% Catholic and 100% voodoo. She looked at me briefly without comment. "You'll learn quietly that the natural and the supernatural live hand in hand. To locals, strange things go along fine – all the better for being unexplained. Like the 'undertaker wind', for instance."

"What's that?"

"A night wind that blows from inland out to sea, prophesying death. It comes without warning."

"Is this suicide mentoring?" she laughed.

"No, not at all."

"But you condone my ambition? Where did you read about death winds?"

"I forget. But I thought you might like to explore the supernatural a little."

"That something you believe, enjoy or what?"

"For me it's not a case of enjoy, but of interest. If you believe in it, it changes your outlook. If you don't, it builds a wall between you and what everyone else sees as truth. Most days I hover in the middle – never knowing quite what to believe."

"A steep curve and a paradox."

"I learned, that if you see a thing that fills you with dread, or something that touches you profoundly, you should know it's often there to remind you of life's impermanence. Of the days when the soul aches for lost ideals. The world holds too few signposts. Heed those we get. You should think about it."

"First I need to understand it better. But you're right in a way. This is a day for soul-searching – even if you feel that yours has just been ripped out. But I suppose it makes for good conversation."

I nodded and pulled the sun visor down as we turned fully into the setting sun.

"You suppose right. But why Jamaica?"

"No big secret. A promise Paul made." She sank back in her seat again.

"I can't place your accent, Clark. Where you from?"

"New York, but I studied literature in England for three years. One in Paris."

"That explains it. Never been to England. I'd love to go."

"You should."

We drove out along the foreshore and into more traffic. A wedding convoy held us in line for a while. Ahead, the bride had filled the back seat of the limo with meringue and pink ribbons. She suddenly turned and smiled at us. We both waved back and

laughed. I took us the long way around the point and we motored
on past the quiet, off-season beaches.

"Ever been to Paris?"

"No. Did you visit London?"

"Many times."

I saw her react. Maybe she was impressed. "I don't mean to
swank it up, Case, you understand. It was just to the British
Library and some equally dusty pubs."

She paused – drifting in thought between me, the road and
Granby. I was pretty sure Granby was still with us in spirit.

"So I know you like a smoke, coconut, beer, literature – all
things Europe. Tell me what you don't like."

She caught me off guard a little, but I decided to try and
answer her.

"Oh, I dislike being a dumping ground. I dislike not having
…"

Case looked at me impatiently. "You mean not having a
girlfriend? Be honest."

I looked back at the road. An open-top car sped past us in a
streak of red. Tanned arms waved in the air as they blew by. We
caught their slipstream.

"I was hard on people for a while, Case. Jamaica showed me
a flow, a process to life. But I guess I'm ready to move on now…
yeah, I'm ready for a girlfriend. Why not?"

"That's a question you need to ask yourself, Clark. Me? I'm
screwed! Sorry to be frank, but I mean that as literally as one can.
Drinks and a smoke might soothe it, but really, what the hell do
I do now? Honestly, he's not coming, is he? And I do not believe
in the probability of later. I've got just two nights left at my hotel.
Christ! The whole damned trip was on him."

Case looked at me in deep frustration.

"I need a break, Clark. I've been marooned. Paul was
supposed to . . . We were planning new lives for ourselves here.
It wasn't just a fling. At least, I thought so. Now I'm desperately
low on funds. What the fuck? I can't go back."

"Be gentle on yourself for a day or two. Then ask those questions again. You'll have some ideas." She looked displeased at my suggestions.

"I know it sounds trite – but trust life a little. Believe me. Things will come right soon enough."

"Do you mean lean on luck, Clark?"

"Look, something will turn up. It usually does."

"I could light bonfires to passing ships, I suppose."

"I'd be careful of ships which make passes."

"Ha ha!"

A sign for Harbour Views high on a lamp post had me steer for the middle lane.

"Do you know The Bristol? Only I think we've turned off too early. Mind, there is one thing I love about staying there. The frozen cocktails. Biggest you've clapped eyes on."

I caught her presence then, a spark of something. I'd not felt this way about a woman for a long time. But why this girl?

"Clark?"

"Sorry, miles away. Yeah, I know the hotel. White frontage. Columns. Looks like a bank."

"It's past this garage — next left."

We swung wide and I turned into a tree-lined avenue.

"God! I'm feeling tired now." Case said with a sigh. She wound the window down then fanned herself.

"Want me to pull over?"

"No. I'm all right. What do you do at DALCO?"

"Bulldozing, ore removal – in fact pretty much what I'm told to."

"Sounds like hard work."

"Not too much. Six months on, a month off. We bunk free. Canteen's cheap – finish early Fridays and I get every other weekend off. Oh – the pay's pretty good."

"Hmm, ore mining – is that idyllic? Full of coincidence? Bulging with superstition?"

I laughed. "You'd be surprised. Here, the supernatural is all around us. It's a fact of life. Even at the mine."

"You're intrigued by fact and fiction, aren't you? But it is impressive hearing about the tribal past of Jamaica. I wish I'd read something about it. Funny how people just dash off somewhere because it looks hot and idyllic, with all sorts of fun things to see and do but never take a blind bit of notice to try and see what's underneath the surface. I guess every place has an undercurrent, doesn't it?"

"It's not just the past. It's here in the present. There are scarred and painted bone men, witchdoctor barons who make powders and potions to make you swoon or maybe heal you. There are deep caves with fetish totems, worshipped and wetted with chicken blood during Santeria. There are …"

"OK! Stop! Now you're trying to frighten me with voodoo."

She pursed her lips, gathered her long hair and unconsciously pulled it over her left shoulder. "My life was messy enough before I came to Jamaica, Clark. I studied in Wisconsin. Got an engineering degree. I was the only female on the course. Fought tooth and nail to get it. Paul was my tutor. Maybe you guessed?"

"Nope."

"Well, we hit it off soon after I'd shown him that I could beat his other students. I suffered for it afterwards, though. Guys thought I earned my grades on my back."

I nodded empathically, best I could, but I wished I could steer her off talking about being on her back with another man.

"Look, you're not marooned – you're on liberty. Think of it like that. You must have enough for a week or two – haven't you? It's not all bad. Nothing ever is. Forget home life!

Not paying enough attention to the road, I suddenly swerved to miss a parked vehicle. Case smiled and motioned for me to watch the traffic. I kept quiet until we hit the next intersection.

"Tell me, if you like mystical things, Case, there are lots of places to visit."

"Are we back to superstition already?"

"Kind of."

"Well, is there any message for the marooned? An Astrological prediction perhaps?"

"Oh, don't get me wrong, I'm no expert. I'm not a seer or anything like that. But you'll find a bone woman if you ask around enough. I know a miner whose mother is an Obeah."

"Wow, are those connections useful? I do feel the need for a window on the future."

I felt the rawness of her comment. There was more than just a hint of sarcasm in it – but taking the day's events into account, I was doing well to distract her at all.

"Case, we are in an uncanny place. You just need to open your eyes to it."

The traffic filtered away and so did the trees. We entered a long, deserted avenue where the white curbstones shimmered on either side of the road. The wavering white lines converged in the far distance. I drove dead centre of the road in silence. It was past sundown now and the lawn sprinklers had come on — some were jetting across the pavement. A passerby walked round the overspray. I felt the slight crackle of the report paper nestling in my pocket. I wondered if I should simply pull over and read the damned thing. Case turned and eyed me carefully. Porch lights were flickering on now as we drove by these elegant homes with their high front stoops sitting above a perfect square of grass. Soon, this street would be busy with party traffic. Several of the biggest clubs in Kingston were on the outskirts of this district.

"Do you actually like the island, Clark? Got a favourite place?"

"Yes! But I prefer life on the North side. I live in Ocho Rios, in St. Mary's. A very beautiful parish. Midway along the eastern shore there's a shallow lagoon, near Falmouth, where a strange luminous plankton grows. If you row out at night and trail your hand through the waters, the lagoon lights up an eerie blue-green. Catch it and the rainbow fires mingle in your fingers. They go out as quickly as the water escapes your hands. But after the light vanishes, it reappears at the tips of your oar blades or at the skip of a stone on the surface. Swim there and the soft muds pull at your feet like quicksand. I've heard some say they'll snatch you under in a whisper. Here, the unnatural is as real as the natural."

Case gave me a cold look of disbelief and opened the glove compartment.

"Need something?"

"I'm looking for the guidebook you get this stuff from," she smiled.

I pulled into the forecourt of the Bristol Hotel. A double line of thick-trunked palms sat in carefully painted white-stoned islands. We stopped in their shade. "Home sweet home," I said. "Now, try to enjoy your weekend. Don't think too much about Granby." Her head flicked round. She climbed out then leaned back in to grab her bag from the footwell. At that point she smiled at me — a wonderful, bright, warm, intelligent smile that raised my spirits. It's all I'd wanted since the moment I met her. I was moved by it.

"I'm in Kingston from time to time. I'd like to take you to Brady's."

She paused before answering me. Her silence was telling.

"Not been there. Any good?"

"Local foods – on the beach – night fires – calypso music, sea views."

More silence . . . She turned away.

"I *might* like that", she said, without looking back.

Chapter 2

A first time for everything

In the months that followed, I only saw Case every other weekend. Our Saturday evenings on the beach at Brady's became a staple. So much so, I worried that too many sunsets had dampened our start. It felt like we were in a never-ending final scene of a movie, one without a whirlwind beginning or a thrilling middle. We always met at dusk — never in the full light of day — and I swear there was something vampiric in that. Later, we took to meeting halfway between Kingston and St. Katherine's.

We hung out at the Bristol on Sunday afternoons, where Case drank the biggest frozen daiquiris that I'd ever set eyes on. Fortunately, her father — under protest it seemed — sent funds from home. Along with the money came a fierce begging letter which ordered her to return the moment the dollars ran out. After a few weeks, I helped with a small loan. We scoured the Daily Gleaner for jobs in the evenings and Case finally managed to find work in a bar called *The Better Half.* Whether she took the name as an omen or a revenge mantra, I don't know, but it helped sustain what life she had. When I picked her up on a warm work night, I'd kiss her cold lips and taste cherry and spiced maraschino.

Case Robins was feisty in the early days of our relationship. She wouldn't put up with any low-ball shots from me. Not that I blamed her for that. I could be more than a handful of trouble at the best of times. The fire cat emblem I'd tattooed on her personality faded slowly. But I guess it faded at the same rate as I reformed. In the main I found her loving, kind, honest and more than satisfying in and out of bed. The first time I explored her body was after we'd eaten a delicious meal in the cheapest of jerk shacks, somewhere on the road between Ocho Rios and Boscobel. She'd pulled my left hand from the gear stick and put each of my fingers in her mouth – just as slowly and as lasciviously as she could. By the time she got to the fourth finger, my head was spinning. I leaned forward to kiss her, then heard the tyres squeal and in sheer panic, I stalled the engine. We came to a rolling stop. I took a deep breath, frowned, then urged her to walk the rest of the way down to the beach with me. On the steep path there was a slight breeze coming off the sea which caught gently in her hair and dress. When we came to the sands, we took off our shoes and lay down in a dip between the ocean and a grassy verge.

I kissed her for a while on the darkly lit beach, only coming up for air when I felt the deepest urge to climb on top of her. But with her legs wrapped around me she had a strong hold of my waist. So I hugged her closer. Then, between keeping an eye out for late-walking couples or tide hawkers, I rather untidily pushed my hand inside her shirt to fondle her breasts. After a short while I could see her smiling at my attempt to excite her. I continued, but I knew my nerves were showing now. Case tugged her shirt straight again and sat up.

"It's still too cold for skinny dipping – isn't it?" She laughed.

A change of pace, but I fully understood her.

"Yes – still too cold. Let's wait a month."

Suddenly she grasped me again and kissed me hard. Her hair fell over my chest and I felt her hand pulling at my belt. "I thought . . ."

She broke away for an instant. "I was testing you – you idiot! At least you are some sort of gentleman under all the bravado."

I had imagined this moment for too long. Now it was here and she was in front of me. I stroked her hair from her face and we sat up close to each other. The moon was full on the water. The slow lap of waves sounded distant and unreal. We had no blanket and the sand on her skin shone bright silver. She kissed her way down my chest until her head rested near my lap. But biting my lip, I rolled her over. "Look, don't you think we'd be more comfortable at my place?"

"I don't want you to have to drive me back in the morning, Clark. Come to mine. You can go straight to work from there after breakfast."

Her small lodging in a disused *cell* of the Bristol was cramped but solved the problem perfectly. The manager had used it himself when he first came to Jamaica more than nine years ago. Case had fixed it up a little and it looked homely enough. I bounced up onto the bed while she slipped out of her dress. I couldn't take my eyes off her. She had a beautiful, slender form and full breasts. Case climbed up beside me and I unhooked her bra. Kissing my way down her neck, I took each pink nipple into my mouth and delighted in sucking them tenderly. Then, squeezing her tightly, I pulled her up towards me. But she pushed me away and lay back down. I locked eyes with her. I could feel her heat. Her gaze intensified as I kissed my way over her breasts again and then over the taught, smooth stomach. She was breathing hard now as I ran my fingers over the wells beneath her ribs and down over the crest of her hips, exploring every valley and undulation. There was nothing of her I wanted to miss. I delved deep between her thighs and buried my face in her until finally, she lifted my head. It was the first time I'd tasted her; the first time I'd felt she really was mine. I still remember her powerful insistence as she flipped me over and pushed herself down on me. The speed of my entering her caught in my throat and I gave a low moan.

It wasn't the best sex we've had – not by a long chalk – but it had that trepidation about it, where the death of so much fantasy met the stark reality of her being naked in my arms. Her real warmth, her actual scent; the tingling sensation of her fingers moving over my body that had brought our bliss to life. The sound of the cicadas outside the window zinged in our ears afterwards, made worse by the excitement which stayed with me for some time. She tidied the bed and climbed under the covers leaving one long leg outside, hoping to stay cool. Of course, things were not all roses and wine after that. Life never is — but it was the start of something very fine. However, without any real vacation time, we both soon began to tire of the same places and routines.

One Sunday we drove back to Palisadoes, to the old fort at the tip of the causeway. We passed Jacob's Bar on the way through, but Case didn't want to go in. Frankly, that puzzled me. She was as much a sentimentalist as I was. The trip also bought back memories of Thorne and Sansano. Thorne's crumpled report was part of a detailed conclusion. The main rock types were listed as striated and rested at dip of 60 degrees with vertical and asymmetrical fault planes. I had discussed all this with a foreman, but he said the thing was incomplete and even though it hinted at dangers I should put it out of my mind. DALCO would have the full report and I should leave it to experts to determine if the bluff was safe from a slide or collapse - pre, post or during mining activity. So that's how I left it.

Arriving at Fort Charles, we marched through the imposing black steel gates under a bleached-bone sky.
Case went up onto the 'quarter deck' and sat astride a 60lb cannon. She leaned forward to look through the crumbling gun port.
"We're quite far from the sea here. Not much of a lookout."
"The harbour's all changed. Silted up, years back. But you're safe from attack."
"Am I? What if it's an inside job?"
"Not from this angle," I said. I lifted her into my arms and swung her down off the cannon.
"My, that's one big gun," she jested.
I smirked. "Yes. But it's out of action. Sadly retired."
I kissed her and we took the steps down into the courtyard again. We stood under a tall palm that grew next to the main blockhouse turned museum. The trim, white-painted walls were all 'terribly' ship-shape.

"People defend the things they love, don't they?" Case said suddenly.

"Empires come and go." I said.

"But there's always a choice, Clark." By now I was lost. I had no idea what she meant by that. In fact, most of the things she'd said to me that morning seemed random or double-edged in some way. She'd acted oddly yesterday, too. I glanced at her. Case was in another world.

A breeze blew up at noon as we walked to the Giddy House, a half-sunken munitions store outside the fort. A large Ceiba tree had grown up against it. I told her that spirits of the dead were thought to live in these sacred trees.

"They say if you let one grow by your home, the spirits will throw heat down on you."

I stopped to take some photographs. Case went on ahead, firmly holding her straw hat. I was caught in her mood and sensed a storm coming. I went inside and stood on the sloping floor, fighting the incline that tipped me toward her. Out of the sun, I suddenly felt a damp chill. Case slumped heavily away from me against the back wall. She removed her hat and stared upwards.

"He's written to me, Clark. Paul Granby."

"I see."

"Do you? Not long or involved. Says he's coming over. Asked how I was. What I was doing. Sorry he hadn't heard from me – you know, all that kind of thing." I paused to take it in.

"So that's why you are a little off today. Well, I suppose the fool's waited a long time. Too long I'd say. Now you're going to reply, to tell him?"

I crossed the floor and lay back on the sloping wall next to her, our faces caught in the rising light from the open windows opposite.

"About us?" she said. "Not sure. I don't know *what* to do, Clark."

"Well, it looks like we've hit a place as crooked as this one. And all of a sudden? Tell him nothing."

"You mean, does he need to know? Just give him the —"

"I don't know. I've not had time to think. Just write a few words to him. The fewer the better. Tell him not to come."

"He's coming this week. I've had the letter for days. I didn't know what to do with it. I was going to bring it with me but …"

"But? Look, Case, I don't need to read it. Just reply, for Christ's sake, before he takes the plane."

"But what have we got? I mean, actually… What are we, Clark? He could be a *lifeline*." I didn't like the sound of that one bit. I thought I already 'owned' the lifeboat. The fact that Case had kept this to herself for so long was hurting me. I thought I was worth more.

"Case! I ought at least to be told about things that could wreck us or cut me adrift. Do you still love him? Well, do you?" I said harshly.

"Don't shout at me, Clark."

"Well, why lay this on me out of the blue? You have known about it for some time. You just said so. Don't I matter? Can't I help?"

She never replied. She just stared at the floor. I tried to cool off. We both looked up through the glassless windows into the sky. The wind ruffled her hair. Another couple strolled in. I think they detected an atmosphere, because right away they tip-toed out again.

"Look, it's taken me a week to tell you this."

"You picked a nice day."

"I need to know – are we important to each other, Clark?"

"Case! You really want to do this here? Now? I thought we'd pledged togetherness – haven't we? Or is that too tribal for you? What do educated moderns do these days? Throw engagement parties? Is this why we avoided Jacob's? Because it reminded you of him, or meeting me — or something else bad? Just reply to Paul and tell him you're seeing someone. Tell him the guy you're seeing might not be the man of your dreams – but he's a darn sight less complicated – and he *loves* you, very much."

I turned to look at her. A smile brightened her face. I guess she was pleased I'd finally said it. I hadn't planned to. Not here, not like this. But I did love her and just then I was suddenly afraid to lose her. The wind chased around the walls and I could hear it buffeting the silk cotton tree outside. I shivered slightly. She smiled, put her hat on me and rolled into my arms. I felt her weight shift. Her firm breasts pressed against me. We kissed and hugged tight for a while.

"Do you mean it?" she said.

"Every word."

"It was nice of you to say it properly, with meaning, for the first time," she whispered. Clark, I need stable ground. More than a pledge. Do you understand?"

I stroked her hair and face lightly.

"I'm sorry I took so long about it. But Granby's no lifeline – no life at all. We need to tidy these loose ends – don't we?"

"Yes, I do. And you have."

"Mean it? You're done with him?"

"I am."

"All right. Anything more?" She looked up with a coy smile on her face.

"I've just said it, haven't I?" I let it hang.

"Sure . . . then write to him today."

"All right." I felt her kiss my cheek.

"I don't want – I don't…" I couldn't find the words.

"It's messy, Clark. He's a sticker. I tried to give him up before, but it didn't work. He keeps coming back. I'll probably have to call him. But what if he won't let me go?"

"He will. If not, I'll call his wife. I'll call the college to report misconduct. Then I'll call him."

"You'd do that?" I squeezed her tighter.

"I'll bury him under a thousand tons of bauxite if he comes here gunning for you."

"Really? I see Fort Charles has woken a warrior."

She kissed me on the cheek again, then pulled away. I let her go, feeling slightly relieved. I eased my shoulder off an old iron hook that was digging into me. Water pooling against the back wall reflected white sky and the three open brick windows turned to choice escape routes from the musty brick cavern. The wind had died a little now. I gave her back her hat, pressing the thing hard onto her untidy head. She went outside alone, leaving a trail of damp footprints on the cement floor. The Giddy house had half sunk into the ground in an earthquake centuries ago. Likewise, her news today had sunk my heart and jolted my world more than she knew. I guessed I would just have to trust her. I'd shown my hand. I'd told her I loved her. She'd hinted at feeling the same way, but I guessed that Granby still stood between us. Until she'd banished him for good, it was my turn to be in limbo.

Chapter 3

A Past Life

Before meeting Case, I'd lived in a kind of self-willed ignorance and was guilty of the sin of delayed adolescence. Now if that sounds like a small crime – it isn't. I liked childish things and had childlike rebellions. I had childish tantrums too. And, like a child, I forgot the nasty things that I said to people too easily, making no mention of them again. Not to anyone. But the people to whom I spoke nastily remembered. Subsequently confronted, I was generally on the back foot. Then I went away feeling rather ashamed and embarrassed about my big mouth, my bullish bravado. I wondered why I had said all those things. My father told me once that when youth meets high ideals and lacks responsibility, irresponsibility follows. But really, it wasn't that complex. I simply blamed others for my fallen opportunities. I dumped my insecurities and simple artistic failings onto the people I loved. I had little else to do with my internally brewed poisons. But a certain restraint entered me when Case was around. I quickly learned a lot about myself from my relationship with her and also from my friends on the island. She had re-formed my tongue and spoonfed me my adulthood.

After our talk at the fort, a vital energy sprung from Case. She worked hard to make our lives fun and adventurous. She introduced me to obscure, ridiculous things — such as extreme treks to distant mountains where we sipped madly strong coffees whilst sitting on top of ancient mounds. The Arawak natives had celebrated rites here. There were legends of great deeds in the Blue Mountains and they say it was on the summit that boys became men. We shared more than advancement and new ideals. Those things went on beneath the surface, while we laughed at maddeningly silly things, discussing equally maddening drinks as we drank them. We supped all kinds of fruit wines, potions, liqueurs and secret remedies for extending our sexual bliss. We had fun learning lyrics and words backwards with many silly consequences — especially when we asked for the bill at restaurants. We battled hard on some things but balanced this out with trivial bickering and enjoying each other's idiotic sense of humour. God, how new the world seemed to her. It was as if she was being reborn each day in a different mould; a new paradise unlocked within. I lived hot nights under the palms and golden days filled with red hair, freckled skin and soft kisses. Case loved a thousand pursuits and she made them infectious. We rented out boats at weekends and lazed in flat calms, barely worried if we'd ever get back. Other days we lay in bed all morning and watched the geckos race across the walls, and the sun move through the room in a haze of yellow. We walked the cliff tops at Morgan's lookout and sat, legs over the edge, with the wind rushing up from the slopes and the gulls screeching in our ears. We laughed and fed each other wild berries while searching the forests of St. Mary's for ruined sugar plantations. Case stopped to gaze at the rusted cogs and broken boilers littering the grass around the old mills. We sat down in the great iron cauldrons which had melted the syrups and separated the molasses. Under blue-grey skies, we huddled together as tropical storms moved inland across the island. We'd be startled by the flashes of lightning that split the clouds amid rumbling thunder. At other times, we rose at dawn and took a beach picnic and ate fresh melon and coconut washed down with bowls of hot chocolate. The times when she wasn't there, I found that by closing my eyes and relaxing, I could still feel her breath on my cheek. There was so much to experience and to understand about Case. She told me endless stories and I listened, enthralled. Her childhood trips to Canada, her father teaching her to strip engines, the crazy urges of her twin sister… You never really knew what Case might say or do next. She had that odd unpredictability — that sudden eruption of mirth, the edginess and abandon of the natural joy of living that welled within her. Case Robins was very intoxicating.

I'd come to Jamaica to escape the slow building of an isolation cell; self-condemned, as it were. I was heading towards solitary isolation through my own endemic faults. A change of scene throws life into sharp relief. Whatever concerns you might have, a different place angles a new set of problems. My father had kept telling me I was hell to live with after graduation, but I never really listened to him. I never believed him. His oddities propelled my anger. He complicated life with his pseudo analysis of me and his 'life's compass' lectures. My maternal aunt was the same. She fought for my time and pulled me this way and that. After more flaring arguments, I left England and flew back to the U.S. Eventually, unable to live in high self-toxicity with my sister in New York, I took off again. Indeed, maybe to spite Dad's complaints, I stabbed a map of the Caribbean with a compass point. It landed me in the Cayman Islands. The closest hop to a bigger chance of survival was Jamaica. So, one cold September morning, I flew direct from Kennedy to Palisadoes, Kingston. Here I would start afresh. Do something totally unexpected. I had always wanted to write. Now it appealed to me more than ever. I planned new and exotic experiences to feed it. I would transpose to transform.

Before all that, I'd arrived in the UK via Paris, shortly after my mother died. My parents had divorced when I was fourteen. I'd taken up ju-jitsu for four years, enjoying the energy and verve that combat gave, but in general I was no big sports fan. Nor overly hung up about my body image. I wore my hair close-cropped and kept my look in a Spartan, practical style. After I bunked with Dad near London, he got me into Winchester University where I read for my Lit. degree. For three years, I was warm, well-fed and happy — happiest even in the college gardens, among acres of wide meadows and streams that stretched up to Twyford Down. I enjoyed running then and would jog for miles through the Meon Valley. In early May, the trees would burst into bloom and I'd spend hours in the cherry orchards. Here I wrote, testing my iambic pentametre and limping home with my legs still half asleep. Winchester College was a transient pastoral reminder, interned in a post-romantic age. Its whole ambience, a timeless vagueness, was like a slow ticking of an invisible clock that compared to student years, measured without change since time immemorial. John Keats had lived near my college once and I chose to dissect his odes for my dissertation. When I finally donned cap and gown, my critical writing was much improved. Yet destructively, it wound up in cold judgments of myself and of almost everyone else I met: a mortal division of self and intellect. My sister, in her usual, somewhat lengthy manner, had told me that emotional malnutrition leads to the slow starvation of caring for self and others. But maybe she was right? Now that I cared for Case, I felt different.

Aside from writing ambitions, I knew there was more to the move than I'd admitted to my family. I needed to examine what the hell I was going to do with my life; to find out who I wanted to be, or who I was made to be. It's not until you ask such questions that you find the future is an indomitable pressure; a persistent, repelling force, pushing more strongly against you the faster you attempt to climb. Hold your hand out from a speeding car; feel the air push back hard. Turn it palm down and make a knife edge to cut through it. You must fit the future like that. Learn how to hit the least resistance. I never had that skill before the bauxite mine disaster.

After my first three months in Kingston, I headed over to the hills of St Mary's. The parish has some of the best beaches and resorts on the island. I grew my hair. I surfed and I visited some of the townships where I could help kids who couldn't afford college. I advertised in the local paper, *The Daily Gleaner*, for teaching positions and took several jobs; I visited mediocre homes, taught mediocre kids — some in plush residences surrounded by manicured gardens with butler types who served pink lemonade at four o'clock. Before long I'd grown sick of doing bar work in the evening and teaching English to French kids left to rot in Jamaica by their diplomat fathers. I decided I needed a tougher challenge. I'd learned to drive forklifts and baggage trucks at Gatwick during my summers off from university. So, when I heard that DALCO needed big CAT drivers up at St Katherine's, I applied.

Until DALCO offered me the job, I'd never heard of bauxite. Bauxite is a blood-red, mineralized earth used to make aluminum. The earth is extracted and filtered in a complex process. The teams took me in and I learned the ropes quicker than I expected. Under Mike and Mo, I tackled landfill for six months, giving the guys a real shock at how much I cared for the great yellow iron beasts. We infilled exhausted seams and replanted the landscape. The work suited DALCO's ecological spin, complying with some of the new laws which were being passed to return land to its original state. DALCO most often paid rent for land and then handed it back to the landowners after processing. Our restoration practice was aimed at supporting its application for new licenses. At first, we were not part of the mining community. We were just hired hands, run by DALCO foremen. Two of the foremen came from Chapel Hill, Texas. One was Mr. Jake Krebbs. You only got overtime from Krebbs if you scratched his back with dollar bills.

The work took place in all weathers, on various shift patterns from dawn until dusk. First, we rolled and spread gypsum on rested waste deposits. Then I worked front-end loaders: big, rusted, badly dented contraptions, built in the late '80s. Although we kept hearing investment was due, there was no sign of it. I moved to grabbers next under Mo. Loading the ore was testing work, but Mo taught me to walk, spin and pirouette those machines like no-one else. The machine literally came alive in his hands. Later, we went on to training new men on the CATs. Big Mike Jakana was our crew's leading hand. He had a special way with teams, settling men into neat routines quickly. He also initiated me into mining parlance and drove me crazy with his hints and advice on everything from setting a tool belt to hydraulic compression and cleaning down equipment properly.

Mike was the right arm of our team. I couldn't have done the job without him.

Things carried on much the same with Case after our agreement at the Fort. The next week she had telephoned Paul, only warning me at breakfast the very morning she was going to do it. I stopped her between mouthfuls of toast before I left.

"Don't we have some unfinished business?"

"What kind?" she asked, washing her half-chewed toast down with coffee.

"The pledge kind? From the fort? I have waited, Case. Am I just a lifeboat that takes you from one guy to another?"

"No. I love you, Clark," she blurted. It seemed too off-pat to be true or given with any real feeling. But she saw the look on my face and read me easily. "I do mean it Clark," she said softly. "I do. I just want to put Paul Granby behind me first. OK? Now is that all our unfinished business done?"

"It is," I said reluctantly.

"You only had to ask."

"Well… I wanted it to come from you… but you don't sound -" She stopped me from talking by pulling me down to her and pressing her lips tightly against mine. I relaxed, before standing away, smiling rather idiotically as I recall.

All day I felt nervous about her call to Granby. It was very late that evening, when we were sitting in Clay's having supper, and in between bites of goat's cheese, bread and sips of sparkling wine, she told me about his protests and her announcements. She'd told him straight she was involved with me and not to fly in. I'd felt more relieved by that than I ever imagined. And by her account she'd handled him pretty well. Yet at first, I wasn't sure if the affair really *was* over, although Case insisted it was. To be honest, I half expected him to turn up any day. However, as the weeks passed it seemed less and less likely. At times it crossed my mind that I was blinded by my love for Case, and that I was missing something important — like the signs predicting that a man would come to kill our love. Were those signs still there, but invisible to me on the wind?

Was I being played for a fool? After all, I'd only known Case for a short time. Such thoughts simmered until all talk of Paul Granby had dissolved into the ocean like a bitter pill. With patience, our lives settled down and eventually I invited Case up to dine, 'on campus' as it were. It was from there she became interested in looking for a job at the mine.

Chapter 4

The Bauxite Mine

When Case joined DALCO, I'd just made shift supervisor. They gave her a lead in retooling, admin and scheduling. She settled in fast and pioneered the crew's Friday nights out at Magrite's, a local venue for live music. Really, it was just a dirt yard behind a small hutch — the bar — with dodgy electric power tapped from passing overhead cables. Case astonished me how quickly she gained a technical understanding of the Bayer process, surpassing some of DALCO's foremen. Her engineering knowledge was also keyed into production and residue recycling. I was so proud of her, and she was well respected by the crews. Like me, she became reliant on Mike, Mo and the other girls. We both enjoyed being in company now, almost as much as we did spending time alone together.

Ever since the crew became prime-time DALCO men, our new status brought perks. We could bunk in the camp huts now, so one night at Margrite's we decided to apply to bunk together. Mike had hooked up with Anne Martine, Mo had met Juanita and I was madly in love with Case Robins. Our proposed arrangement brought its challenges and its rewards. But I got to know my crew's passions well and perhaps more notably, their foibles and frailties too . . .

Take Mo for instance; an odd kid who grew up in Dale on a hilltop farm owned by his mother. His father, long dead, was a Maroon who married out of Scots Hall town. I fear they'd had Mo too late in life. Mo was full of innocent drives and speculations on the world — rather like my own — before education had dissolved their potency. Men have clung to worse ideals, but in Mo I saw the curiosity we have about reaching for the stars slowly disappear. A life-blood, that only the cynic or the magus steals away, ebbed from him daily. He did little or nothing to fight back against the forces of his mother's superstitions and pseudo-religious beliefs. Here, a balanced hand is required to bring a fresh outlook. But it was a hard thing to help him with, a harder thing to offer too. It saddened me that Mo's family drove the devil's bargain on him. But I find that a passive force — such as doing nothing, feeling nothing – powers a negative. Nothing forms its own beggared lair and loss procreates where nothing lives. Mo's gradual loss of belief in and understanding of modern life was a shameful thing to behold. Like I said, it was sad to see him dried up and aged, like so many elder trees, with a bitter reticence for growth and change. Yet in the gladness of talk, our friendship withstood the rising tides. I liked Mo. I enjoyed our conversations. After hours, he taught me calypso songs passed down from his grandfather and he also showed me how to eat 'local', especially a blackened dish of spiced chicken – 'Jerk' they call it. That was his favourite. He also flooded me with reggae. I'd shown little or no interest in reggae music before I landed here, but on Jamaica the sound quickly imprisons you.

My ore removal crew relied most on Anne Martine, who set the shift rosters and tonnage estimates. I got to know Anne more slowly than the others. She was a Texan, from a big wealthy tribe of dysfunctional relations. They'd owned land once flush with oil, but by the time the wells had dried up, the water rights had all been sold. Now there was no going back to the dustbowl left them, and when roots are withdrawn, we cannibalise any growth achieved. Anne at times shrank away from herself and her duty to others. I noticed something else too — something pained about her that tied Mike's girl off from most. Maybe it was her childhood ideals, long abandoned before DALCO had entered her life. Or maybe she was just disconsolate like the rest of us; a wind-blown spirit taking on the colour of the land wherever it settles. Anne was tainted in that way by her friendships. She enjoyed a love-hate relationship with Mo's girl, Juanita, whose job in the canteen was where Mo's love of jerk gained an epicurean appreciation. That said, our rough diamond of a gang gelled well. We slotted together like pieces of a jigsaw filed down to fit. Ours was not clean work, but it was hard and honest work. We cut seams, danced wild nights away, moved ore, retooled, got paid, ate, loved, fought and laughed together.

The mining operation was 'plein air', opencast. A British-Canadian effort. We stripped off the topsoil and overlying deposits (the overburden) then removed the mineralised earth to grade it. The ore was processed at the camp in three main stages: crushing, to increase the surface area; removal of chemical impurities and then, after being turned into slurry, digestion. For that, the mix was pumped into hot caustic soda tanks where gibbsite and other minerals dissolve to form a 'pregnant' liquor. The end product is shipped off the island. Bauxite's final processing uses vast amounts of electricity to form aluminum, so Jamaica exports only the 'pregnant liquor' or a calcined crystal.

Mining bauxite leaves a by-product, a sludge, a red toxic mud that sits in man-made lakes. Some of these blood lakes hold millions of gallons. They sit out in virgin forest, as far as the eye can see — far away from the cities and settlements. They either dry out to form red dust clouds in the summer or burst and flood the land and rivers with toxic minerals after the rains.

Bad health dogged everyone at the mine. After a day's work, we came back dyed red from head to toe; hands, face and clothing stained blood red. My hands suffered the worst. *The Daily Gleaner* reported often on the number of ailments that bauxite miners endured, including cancers from radioactive minerals causing permanent disfigurement. I scrubbed hard at my hands and face every day, wondering if any of these elements had leeched under the skin and got into my blood. Krebbs was always washing his hair and complaining of a blocked nose. Fortunately, I had very dark brown hair — almost black — and there was not a dye that could touch it. For the rest, we set aside the stories of rare earth-poisoning, acute asthma and mental breakdowns – to tick a few more off the Gleaner's list. But mostly it was the dust that bothered us – the raw, red-blooded dust from the shallow seams that changed the landscape and our skin. On dry days, red dust clouds rose into the sky and hung there, floundering in the hot air. As the evening cooled, the dust settled and caught in the throat. It turned the palms and faces of all the workers red. You could hardly breathe amid the iron thickness of it all. Near the mine, the sea turned red where red rivers ran from the cliffs. And all the trees and all the roads turned red too as our rusted earth gave its blood for aluminum.

The wooden huts that we bunked in were built way back when. Row upon row of them, arranged like those old pictures of concentration camps. When we first moved in, we tumbled around enjoying the booming echoes from the old boards. The huts rested on stilts perched on Blue Mahoe stumps to keep the floors from rotting. Blackened by sun and rain, the clapboards were buckled and the joists bowed. Close-up, burled knots stood proud on the planking like the calloused knuckles of a boxer. I guess we were cramped and hot inside, but not miserable. The sharing was all we could have hoped for; cosy in the dead of night when the sky was so full of stars you would see their reflection like an overspill on placid lakes and calm lagoons..

A cool breeze swept up from the bay and blew through our dorm, more often than not. It was almost pleasant inside the hut at that time, and somehow the dust hardly managed to get in. The beds were uncomfortably hard that first winter, but we'd got cotton-filled mattresses in spring and they proved better than the straw ones which had stayed damp and smelled bad after the rains. In October, the worst of the storms hit us with hurricane force. The wind blew so hard you could literally lean fully into it and not fall over. The huts shook in the storms and the stout beams groaned like beasts caught in steel-jawed traps. Rain here sounded like a million ball bearings drumming on the roof and against the windowpanes. The walls of the huts were not straight or true; everything had bowed, from the great joist up to the eaves. The trusses in the open roof space, with all its jointed wood and the heavy crossbeams — and even the floorboards — had all been warped by nature in some way or another. We had a rule of course: no boots in the hut but standing in the pouring rain to remove them was cold and tedious and it soon became an erstwhile pursuit. I'd never seen or heard downpours like it. The rolling thunder, coupled with the noise of the machinery, gave us little peace. Our hut was number one of twelve, situated the furthest south. Backfill of sector nine began around March and we'd come off shift by the end of the month.

Despite our persistent bouts of influenza, we lingered on and slept through April with our girlfriends. A venturing six: Anna and Mike, Juanita and Mo, Case and me. The jilted and the jaunted washed in from shores on unpredictable tides. Early one morning we painted a board and renamed the place: '*The Six Doubloons*'. Case and I broke a bottle of Holsten Pils over the plank before we hung it. Mike raised a glass and gave us two good choruses of 'La Vie En Rose.'

Our dorm for a year was this sixty-foot log cabin, a wooden 'super liner' from an age before steam. Oblong and divided easily, stable-stall style. The heavy wooden dividers fell just short of the main roof truss. Privacy drapes were drawn across the front of our billets and bottles would roll easily under these drapes; beer, wine, cordials, whisky and the like would travel the full uneven length of the shed, and we would often not know whose drink was whose. And it was too easy to kick a bottle flying so you had to be careful to put all the empties back in the crate to avoid breaking glass on the bare floor. Two berths along from Case and me, in the 'spare' stall, was our bathroom. This backed onto Mo's berth. We also had a shower block which was shared with two other huts outside. Nearest my bunk, by the entrance, was a small extension with an old butler sink, fridge and hob. We shared some home comforts here: a bottomless coffee pot, a larder, crammed mostly with beers, a variety of fruit breads and jerk sauces. There was nowhere to wash clothes, so we used the company laundry service. Sometimes they pressed my sleeves inside out, for reasons unknown both to me or the laundress. Smokes were cheap at the canteen and the food spicy and hot. We weren't cosseted, but we were happy. It wasn't a first-rate hotel, but there was an exceptional beach below us and we had magnificent views over the Caribbean Sea. No flu could deter us. But I guess Case and I passed the flu germ back and forth for weeks. All through April, I suffered with persistent colds and feverish aches. During the night, I shivered for long periods and cried out, occasionally waking the others. The only remedy here was more blankets and bottles of Paracetamol. It was convenient and polite for Case to put it all down to a 'kissing' bug, whereas I'd put it down to sex: more accurate by far. None of us could give it up. Case was too damned beautiful and too damned seductive to be more than moments away from a lingering, dutiful 'kiss,' to use her word. Like moths to flame, we made love for the endless thrill of it.

Case could not be compared to oval Vogue-era faces; nor matched to film starlets, vintage Hollywood dames or even the classic beauties of fine art. There was nothing in Case of Antonio Canova, apart from her translucent skin that shone like fine marble in certain lights. My Case Robins was like pure Impressionism. You could picture her a hundred times from the same angle in different moods, and never pinpoint exactly what it was that made her so beautiful to look at. She was approachable much of the time, with a Cubist heart that understood you from all angles. An hour with her enabled you to take her in without a single secret spoiling the effect. Picasso swung in her palettes of emotion and she lived intensely, through cerise silks, mint-green cottons, buttercup yellow dresses and blue indigo jeans. Matisse owned a swag or two of her hair, which trailed in cut-paper shapes down her back or piled in minarets above her long sensual nape. If you studied haute couture, you might agree that Case even transcended the quirky creatures adopted by the fashionistas or photographers mining for photogenic DNA. She blended

modernity with simplicity and a caring touch. Case was 'a priori'
— a previously known principle — created from the perfect
form.

Chapter 5

Sign from a Mambo

Mo had been quiet. It was unlike him. He was the noisiest among us. Mo liked to hum a calypso, eat jerk chicken or smoke ganja — preferably all at the same time. But his favourite pastime was talking. He loved to talk a lot. He talked mostly about calypso, jerk meats, ganja, his mother or his precious CATs. As for me? Well, sometimes I do enjoy conversation with people who need a good talking-to. But I was busy idling in bed when Mo turned up that morning.

"Yoh! Awake?"

"Mean me?"

"Yeh. Letter from my mother, Clark."

"Another? What does this one say?"

"She say to make sure we all go to church Sunday. She call us sinners of the worst kind. Say we all livin' in sin here, in sight of the Obeah man."

Mo's mother was never short of instructions. She had a certain way with words that turned them into bitter pills. Any amount was hard to swallow.

"You still listenin' Clark?"

"Yeah – sure go on."

"She say we killin' the earth, killin' the island. She prays for us every night."

Poor Mo, he sounded crushed. His mother's letters were akin to bad religious education seminars, or a feared doorstep visit by Jehovah's witnesses.

"I don't go to church, Mo, and I've never killed anything," I said. "Let alone a whole island. But I've heard blacks tell of our boss as Obeah."

We laughed at that. "Look, it's all rot. Forget it. Honest. Last time you read me your ma's letter, she'd quoted Revelations.

I sat up in bed, my thoughts humming now. "Look, I don't mean to pry but you have to straighten all this out. We've got good jobs here, Mo. They pay well." I waited to hear a reply. He remained quiet. "Okay, fella?"

"Maybe," he said quietly. "My family are God-fearing, Clark. They love this island. They know the rivers turn red when we cut and the sea too. It's plain to see."

Mo spoke in defence of the land and I caught the guttural emphasis. He was upright now, leaning his head against the truss of our hut. I guessed Juanita was out. I thought about the motherly sentiments; such words of kindness, delivered like a Scythian bow! I'd visited Mo's mother just after she'd written her last sermon. It was when Mo got a warning from Don Krebbs. He told him he would fire him next time he missed work without good cause.

"Maybe we are killing the place a little, Mo," I conceded. "A wound or two — but nothing fatal. You could always move out. I'd rather you didn't, of course. I mean that. I like what we've got here. It's rare to find such a good crew who can all muck in without too much drama."

"I understand, Clark, but everything here is leading to a bad something. I can feel it. Perhaps she right. We make bad Loa."

I knew what he meant by that, about bad spirits and all that – but I couldn't believe in demons that meant us ill-will. I loved reading about superstitions, and I knew you had to respect them, but strong belief was beyond me.

"Witchcraft and magic are used here to bully and to corrupt the truth."

"Mebbe. But don't tell her that!"

I knew Mo's mother was Obeah, or Mambo, as the female priests are called. She was pulling strings to make people dance. I heard Mo pour some iced Ting.

"It's just mud, Mo," I said. "Red earth and water, not blood. There are no bad spirits. We can only heed the warnings that come to us. If we hear a scream on the wind, we should think on it. I do consider signs for the coming of good or bad weather. Some are of some use. Hey… you hear me, Mo?"

"I hear you."

"Okay. Have a smoke. Case has the wisdom weed if you're all out."

I heard the shuffling of foil packets as he searched. Before long, the sweet smell of tobacco mixed with ganja drifted into our flop. I looked up at the clock. It was getting late; nearly 9am. Mo continued smoking between reading his letter over and over and gulping down fresh Ting, a pink lemonade. After a short while, he was back on form.

"Clark! She say I should move into town and walk to work. Now - tell me again, why do I stay here? Why do we, Clark?"

"Because it costs zilch, Mo. And you like the fact we have our girls and the beer and plenty of time to —"

"To rock an' roll?" He cut me short.

"Put that letter away. It tires me thinking about it."

"I think I'm getting the flu sickness. I'm aching like hell, Clark." He paused. "Maybe, I do wants out. These maladies are killing me! Killin' us all." I heard him slump back onto his bed. Mothers can do that to a man.

"Tell Case your woes when she gets back, Mo. You'll get more sympathy there. That's a promise." I switched our talk. "New cuttings open soon. We strip off the overburden early May. Probably take two to three months to prep the bluff. If we moved into town now, we'd still have to share. And it would mean taking a house. Too expensive!"

Mo went quiet, perhaps thinking it over.

Case rattled through the door with Mike. She pulled the curtain aside.

"Welcome back!" I said. "Is it another ugly day out?"

"No, but there is a lot of ash outside. What have you burned?"

"Nothing I can recall. I've just been burning in bed for you."

"I'm serious. There's paper on the step – marked with dark circles and curls – but it's all burned."

Mike continued to his bunk next door. I heard him slide off his muddy boots.

"Shall we start gain? Hi babe. What have you got me?"

"Shopping! We've been into town. You want to go out this evening? I hear a tribute Abyssinians are playing at Magrite's."

She put down the bags and sat on the foot of the bed.

"Nope," I said, watching her deflate a little. "I'm happy just making a song of all this decay. I'm going to write today — if you can lift me out of this smothering rack!"

"Get showered!" She threw a clean towel at me. "And shave!"

"I need a new blade."

"I've restocked on Gillettes."

"I see. What's the occasion?"

"Life – and decency – my health, and modest amounts of self-discipline."

"You are again, *The Golden Mean*."

"And you are a grubby, stale, dark-with-beard, stubble-burning layabout!"

I laughed and heard Mike laugh too. I looked into the great, clear blue eyes tinted with an enviable green iris that changed and flashed, depending on the thousand ways light could play. Their fire shook the daylight from your head and plunged you into dark tropical nights, replete with voodoo drums and loud caterwauling. At least I liked to think so. I suddenly thought again of the paper ash on the doorstep.

"Did the fire outside look deliberate? I mean, was it left there on purpose – not just blown by?"

"I think so. But get up and take a look."

"Maybe I will."

Case turned the page on our wall calendar. Daily she followed an old Farmers' Almanac and always told others how we first met on a Full Wolf Moon. Even now I still howled with hunger for her. The phases were marked along the bottom of the page. Yesterday was a full moon. I put the thought to the back of my mind, climbed out of bed, grabbed the towel and my wash bag and lurched into the washroom.

"Did my Golden Mean buy any chocolate?" I shouted.

"Not for you!"

"How did I guess?"

I got shaved with the old blade then discarded it. Whether she was good or cruel to me, I still called Case my 'Golden Mean.'

"Clark, I'm having a late lunch with Anne. So, canteen for you today. Do you hear?"

"I do hear. I do not like."

And so, my course was set. From the nights of perpetual energy, which flew in the face of scientific laws, where my Case danced like a siren or a demon, to lunching on hard tack with the crews.

We sat back outside together, and I picked through the ash on the doorstep. The half-burned paper was a voodoo sign of some sort. I knew that much.

"The canteen isn't all that bad. You've said that yourself."

"Ah! The sacrifices one makes for women."

"More drama? There's nothing to dislike, Clark!"

"All right then, enjoy lunch," I said. "I'll be fine. Don't worry about me."

"I don't. Now let's get cleared up. We can go to the communal rooms after and at least have more space to 'flop' in."

"What?"

"You used to complain about my hole in the wall at the Bristol. But these flops are half the size."

"Oh, so now it's my fault we are living on top of each other and everyone else here, huh?" I swept a bunch of stuff off the bedside table and put the things down on the bed. I put a picture of Nixie face down.

Born a twin, Case had pinned more pictures on the beams above our bed of her 'Quartered Half', as she called Nixie, than anybody else. Her sister was still enjoying free bed and board at home. Darker-eyed, darker-haired and sullen as a brook in winter (my impression) Nixie was well-to-do, well-fed and all broken in. For me, she was a mirrored half of her sister, but not a quarter as pretty. She was an intern now, at Morgan and Holmes I think, a CAD house in New York. Case had followed her career with singular purpose. And in more wistful airs, I'd catch her sitting quietly as she studiously wrote to her.

Mike poked his head through the drape. "Case! He won't need dat new soap. His skin ain't never gonna be white again. That's a fact. Goes to sho. You unpack the planet, it gonna mark you fo' good." Mike laughed goodheartedly at his own joke.

This was big Mike Jakanna: half-Jamaican, half-Cuban and proud of the fact. He was broad-backed, with a notably sloped forehead, and I'd seen him clear seams for fourteen hours in a frontloader and not miss a beat. He smoked an expensive brand of cigars from Cuba and used a gold clipper too. A man's man. But he spoke true enough. I was a pink shade of red. Case had convinced me it would eventually scrub off.

"We got plenty in common here, Mike," I said, as he wandered off again. "Yo' black, me red and your woman white. Our skin make a flag of all nations," I said, mimicking his accent. Mike snapped his drape shut with a shrug.

As we enjoyed our busman's holiday, my crew, my new *'Chest of Doubloons'* idled on. Beer crates emptied more quickly than the days crept by. Often, the silence was broken only by a box radio set playing over the long, drowsy afternoons. Bottles in hand, we'd sit out on the canteen porch gazing across the palm-strewn slopes to the sea. We'd sit for hours watching the ocean and the ragged, striped cotton sunshields that Case had strung would billow in the warm wind.

Only the locally inbred gloom of unemployment and poverty brooded over the mount. Nothing else spoiled the glow of our vacation. In the slow grind of the passing months, the ensuing poverty had brought growing crowds of protesters up to the gate. Now the dollar was high. The wretched locals were either screaming about pollution or knocking the door down for work. Maybe Craig Sansano wasn't so far from the truth. Maybe one day they would come with torches to burn us out, in some new

Maroon rebellion. But I guessed that as long as we gave them odd jobs from time to time, we'd keep the enemy at bay.

After we'd cleaned, Case set everything back meticulously then stretched herself out on the bed with a sigh. I rolled onto my side. Here, from soft rosy earth, rose softer charms: my Case, with those dark berry lips that pulled you in and teased you and made you think of summers spent when young. I pulled her close to me and pressed my mouth to hers, felt her tongue explore mine. I kissed her deeply and moved my hands over her breasts with as much passion as I could raise. Then I ran my hands down over her warm hips and tugged her towards me. But she fought back, pushing me down firmly.

"For God's sake, Clark," she whispered harshly. "It's almost noon. People are up and about!" My ardour blunted – I felt the rejection. Privacy was an odd concern to have now after being used to my own place and Case at the Bristol. But I couldn't help myself. I loved her. For me it couldn't get any better.

After work it was only a few minutes to this heavenly — albeit decayed — Utopia. We would often lunch nestling in the shadow of a tall cone of rock that jutted out over the ridge. I'd wait there for her to finish her shift, thrilled when she'd grab her stuff, a couple of cold beers, and drag me out of camp. A dry riverbed led down to the beach and we'd pick our way down slowly to where the white sands blazed. At sunset, between the coco palms and red 'Pusstail' shrubs, her hair shone red as a bauxite sun. Deep among the desert roses and azaleas, I made her necklaces of petals.

Further toward the beach at high tide, the cold waves reached a circular hollow where the old stream course had formed a whirlpool. This was our 'divinity tub' and we plunged in over our heads with the chill stealing our breath; love baptised in brine. On the beach, we saw the surf mix with freshwater springs cascading from the ridgetop. We'd walk down after our bathe to paddle in the runnel-scarred sands among the scuttling crabs where visible salt and fresh water blended invisibly. We were like two souls that merge and become one – without ever knowing that they were each a poison to unadapted life? We loved and lived and swam our hearts out there. Further down the coast thundered Dunn's River Falls.

As I changed my clothes I looked at Case — at the sunlight playing across her limbs from the cracks between the planking; at her body curled under the white mosquito nets draped over our bed. Her breasts full, her long legs folded up, knees to chest, like a small child, breathing shallow, quiet, and making me think of times when I had wanted to love a girl so badly, but didn't know how. The things that go untaught to men are those things men most need in life. Like, how does a man kiss a girl so she melts in his arms? How does he balance his anger with his passion? Where does he find the dignity to fight jealousy? And who can tell you such things? Well, I guess now it's just the magic of life, the will to please and the courage to rise above ungentlemanly conduct. Before such wisdom descends, we suffer often and confront the wanting more against the how; such as taking a woman into your heart, marrying her, and knowing well the thrill of her nakedness. Then, across the years, still feeling wrested from the world and heaved up on a tide of bliss, as if it were only yesterday you'd first taken her to bed. Preserved love makes its silent proclamation – oneness. A fact which awakens a striving in me now. Whatever it took to seal our oneness hadn't sprung from me yet, despite the fact we synchronised, Case and I, both without patronage, both self-made poor. As I opened the door again, the vestiges of the paper ash blew across our threshold.

Chapter 6

The Gift of Eyes

Ever since Mo's mother had sent him her first sermon, I'd
wanted to go up to Dale and meet her. I'd heard some say she
was a mambo, a priestess with the gift of eyes; that psychic
intuition which helped her act as an intermediary between the loa
(spirits) and mankind. Her standing in the community was strong.
I decided to make the trip just before our vacation. Back in
March, Mo was a no-show for work three times in a row. Don
Krebbs had threatened to let him go. It was an official warning:
'Mo don't work? Mo no job!' Krebbs was an unpleasant man and
nasty to the locals, be they black or white, but he actually seemed
to enjoy bullying Mo – who was one of the best CAT drivers I've
ever seen. I wanted to know how things had got so bad at home
for Mo, to meet his family; maybe talk turkey with his mother.
Mo's concern was that he'd let the family down. His mother was
always complaining to him that he disrespected the old ways.
These were ingrained, black superstitions that locals lived and
swore by. I had to see where, or if, there was room for a truce.

I caught the regular bus from town, stretched out on the back
seat and opened a Coke. Sunshine streamed through the dust-
streaked windows from a clear blue sky. It was a slow, pleasant
drive along broken roads through overgrown villages and old
shanty towns. White dust trails swirled behind us as we drove
along and hung in the air until we turned out of sight. The sky
arched above the browned hills and the wide valleys spread out
in torpid repose. I sipped my drink and wondered how the forests
clung on to life. I'd seen some farmers willing the rains to come
by throwing powders and magic oils into the wind. Summer had

reached its zenith now. Outside it was the hottest day in living memory.

I knew Mo's father was the son of a Maroon chief; a 'Colonel', now an elected official. The Maroons were an old enemy of the British and I'd read something of their history. They had their own rules, governed in complicated ways. So, I was expecting a tough reception from Mo's family.

After an hour, the driver dropped me at the bottom of a hill. "That way up to Dale," he pointed. I got out and gave my thanks ironically as the doors folded shut and he slowly pulled away. Looking ahead, I pulled my baseball cap around and leaned into the walk. Dale was on a hilltop in a forgotten suburb of Cornwall Parish. The dirt road up was hot and dry. I passed no-one on the steep climb. Across the hillside, all the grass was burned, scorched to straw. Nothing dared flourish here.

When I got up to the house I was out of breath. Blown stalks of straw had caught in my hair and were sticking out of my shirt. Standing opposite the old clapboard front with its rickety porch, I quickly realised why Mo bunked at the mine. Today it was forty plus up here in the shade. I stood there fanning myself with my cap and looked about. There was no patio to speak of – just bleached, dead grass. Glancing back down the road I saw mini cyclones blowing up dust. The tiny swirls zig-zagged up the hillside then hid themselves in the fields. In front of the house a big Alsatian dog lay by the gate. The old boy was panting hard, but he perked up enough to sniff my legs. "Hello, boy," I said, fussing him. "I'm Mo's friend. Easy now." I gingerly edged past the dog. The sun on my back was hot. I noticed the front door was ajar and called out, "Hello? Anyone home?"

Silence followed. "Mo, you inside?"

I turned round and took in the view again. To the south, the valley wandered into the distance bordered by brown, steep hills, in spring these hills shone a tropical verdant green. The sun was directly above the house now and I squinted to look north of the summit. From here you could see acres of sparse countryside dipping into a greener valley to the east. A blue haze hung over

the distant mountains which formed the east-west backbone of
the island. Close by, old timber shacks topped some family
burrows a little way behind Mo's place. A three-bladed windmill
spun slowly next to a broken water tower in the next field.

It was silent, almost creepy here, as if time was suspended and
I was stuck in that odd Wyath painting of the snaked pink girl
looking back at the ghostly homestead. On the slopes, cicadas
chirped above the sound of the wind. I peered inside through the
dust-blown windows. In the glare it was too dark to see anything.
So, I cupped my hands around my face to cut down the light. A
shadow moved in the gloom. Outside, Mo's dog had lain down
again and was looking back at me with one eye open. I shouted
through the open door.

"Mo! Get out here!"

A low guttural voice came out of the dark.

"Who's that?"

"Clark Mason, ma'am. I bunk with Mo at the mine."

An elderly woman shuffled to the door. She was dressed in a
long blue housecoat over a frilled white skirt. She looked at me
wide-eyed, then scratched her chin.

"Ah, the DALCO man. Well, come out back. I got coconut
water, ting or ginger beer. What's your poison?"

"Well, I'm —"

"You wants summin' cold, don't ya?"

"Yes ma'am. Coconut water's fine."

"Hard climb that hill 'bout noon."

"Yeah. I thought the bus came up here."

"Nope. Goin' on six years now. Somebody say it did?"

"Yes. Why did they do that?"

"Aww, they juss foolin'."

I sighed and followed her through the house. A long, thin
room first, with the blinds drawn down, no TV or radio to be
seen. Then on through a beaded curtain into a dining room, all
with lath ceilings, cracked and sepia-coloured. A tiny stairway
curled off to the right halfway through. On the hall walls were
photographs and, in a recess, a small altar set with icons of saints
and white candles. A bell and a small bowl filled with water and

ash topped the chest of drawers, which was spread with a white cloth. I looked at a faded photo. It was inscribed: Kojo day, Jan. 1971. Mo's father was sitting next to his own, celebrating the treaty signed to end the Maroon wars. Next, there was a pinned photo of people river bathing, their hands in the air, all in white wrappings; a cult baptism of some kind. I squeezed past a barrow of vegetables in the pantry and continued into the garden. Narrowing my eyes to the sunlight I saw a small patch of green, luxuriant grass. In contrast to the hill, the yard was well-watered and cool. A wooden side gate had been barricaded with steel hoops, all rusted and tangled together so they resembled a makeshift alarm. We sat down at a table on the grass in the shade of a tall palm. Even sitting still, the sweat ran in rivulets down my neck, back and arms.

"Wantin' Mo?"

"Yep. Can I see him?"

"Nope."

"Oh?"

"Ain't here. Gone see his grandfather. Needs a home talk today."

"Why?"

"Needs to learn more about you and your kind, Mr. Mason."

"Clark, please."

"Needs to be shown our sunny ways; appreciate the life I give him. Ain't no devil taking my boy. Not you, nor others like you. Am I right?"

At that she leaned over and poured fresh coconut water into two blue mugs. She pushed one toward me.

"Thanks," I said, and gulped a big mouthful. It was refreshingly cold with a sharp taste of lemon zest. She smiled and got up easily and went into the pantry. After a while she returned with a tray of frosted-over ice cubes and some mint. She laid the frozen tray in the sun. The ice blanched and cracked loudly.

"Go on, be useful, turn 'em out. My old hands no good with aluminum."

I knocked the tray hard against the table and pressed firmly. The ice cubes tumbled noisily into a jug.

"Help yerself, Clark. Yo not shy!"

"Not shy, just well-mannered – perhaps?"

She took a bone-handled spoon and stirred the drink vigorously. I watched her tear up a handful of fresh mint leaves and add them. The smell of minted ice filled the warm air. She stirred the drink again.

"Manners don't impress me none, when I already know what's inside a man. Ain't no need for pretence here, Clark. Now let me see. Like a piece a melon with ya drink? Gotta a big juicy one inside."

"OK."

She left me for a moment to fetch the melon. Alone I looked around. An old Abeng — a Maroon war horn — hung from a post, abandoned to the elements. Behind me Mo's garden was dominated by a large ackee tree. The dark red pods certainly looked ripe enough to eat. Ackee is both delicious and deadly; it forms part of the national dish in Jamaica. Eaten with saltfish at breakfast, it makes for a bold start to the day. But if eaten unripe, the pods and flesh can cause vomiting, loss of consciousness, fits and even death.

Mo's mother brought a halved melon out on a tray and began slicing it with a steel carving knife. The blade was sharp and steeply arched from long wear and honing on a steel.

"You might take no notice of my ways, Clark, but try to understand how nature works. How God-given life works."

It was clear that she was a bright woman, big-eyed, shorter than Mo, and not exactly as I'd imagined. She'd removed her housecoat now and the simple white cotton shift had puffed short arms with lacy frills. To me there didn't look too much wrong with her hands. I wondered if she was trying to make a point with the frozen aluminum tray. Beside the melon were two ackee fruits. I watched her break them open expertly and slice the ripe flesh away from the pod. The best part of the fruit resembles a fattened grub, or less indelicately, a curled, cooked langoustine. She handed me a thin slice. I showed my reluctance.

"Go on now. It most delicious."

"Thanks." I said quietly. Reluctantly, I took the fruit and chewed it slowly. It tasted nutty, if a little sour in the centre.

"You sure it's ripe?"

"Bin eating it all my life. Ain't died yet." She took two slivers and ate them quickly.

"Mo back soon?"

"Depends on how he takes his lesson."

"Sounds harsh. What's he learning today?"

"Like I said – our ways. Your ways and ours don't always see eye to eye. Mo's grandfather, ol' colonel James, he earned his knowledge. You heard of a Hangoun? He knows best how to pass it on."

"I see. What's a Hangoun?"

"A priest of our ways. My papa - is a cleric of sorts."

"I see. I know Mo loves his family, no-one disputes that, but these lessons, ma'am… they're eating away at him. You've got him so doped he doesn't know which way to turn."

She looked preoccupied with de-seeding the melon now, indifferent to my commentary.

"Do you hear me?" I said. She arranged the slices carefully into a dish and gestured for me to eat.

"You think too much, boy."

"Not too much." I said. "But I'd go so far as to say, poor Mo's half scared to death when he reads your letters to me. I do know you're his mother."

She paused now and looked hard at me. Mo's dog had padded quietly into the garden and had lain down in the shade opposite us. I heard him yawn.

"That's Falco. Mo's dog. Seems to like yo." She mopped her watery eyes gently with a purple handkerchief, then leaned forward on her elbows. "But you don't know me, boy. I do the will of Bondye. I have the gift of eyes. Since a child."

"Bondye? No. But I do know the trouble you can cause for Mo. I've seen what your gift can do. But you *can* use it to do good – so I hear."

"It defend our land." She rasped. "Mo's papa passed when he was a just a boy. Much has happened since that time. We moved here from Accompong. How many years yo lived here?"

"Does it matter?"

"Pah! Tell me, you like this face? I mean this, all around?" She swept her hands through the air. "The hills, the earth, mountains and the ocean?"

"Yes, I like it — very much."

"And the things you don't? Yo treat 'em different?"

"I suppose."

"And what you don't like – you bring hell's fury to bear on. That it? That what yo do when somethin' get in yo way, or to make a fast buck?"

"I don't see what this has to do with Mo's future. Why chain him and lecture him? Why swipe at his dignity? You cheapen his labour and spoil its reward! Mo just wants the respect of his family. He needs it. I think he deserves it."

"Deserves?"

"Yes. He's *earned* it."

"Livin' with people who got sick souls, who make the earth bleed? Is that a way to earn a life? My, if you could tear the face off God you would. If it's a face you don't like? That right?"

A sudden power rushed from her lungs and sliced through me as sharp as the carving knife had cut the red melon flesh. I swallowed hard now with my stomach full of knots

"Like the face of this island," she continued. "Yo cut it deep, Mo cut it deep. Until it all unrecognisable. Many folks come here and do same. Since I was a little girl they come and take our island. They crush it, cut it, then guide our birthright downriver in black boats. Then they load it onto big freighters and thereafter the red dust blows in the wind for a century! I watched them, watched them kill our island with my mama. Now the farmers round here are forced to sell Blood Ore to live!"

"It's good money. We return the land —"

"Money comes, money goes. Nothing *good* about it."

"It's a deal they —"

"Oh! I see the elders from the mount, talkin', dealin' exchangin' their God-given land for red dust. That what they want, is it? They want red dust?"

"Actually, the deal's for aluminum powder. But look, that's in the past. We mine and we earn for —"

"How long Mo know yo?"

"A year plus."

"I say you don't know me or the boy, or our beliefs."

"I know you believe in voodoo. That you summon old gods and press superstition on the young. You use it to turn back the clock, and to honour times past instead of looking to the future, building hope for the young. I've seen you in the flesh now and that too goes a long way to knowing you, don't you think?"

"They're tings that go beyond a physical knowledge of a woman, Clark."

"Maybe."

"All your education!" I looked up as suddenly the palm leaves shook in the wind and their bladed shadows cut across my thighs. I felt there was worse coming . . . much worse. I wondered if I should bow out gracefully before we really came to a shouting match.

"Yo full of hate, Clark, and Ghede coming. I hear him."

She appeared indifferent to the animosity that came from her. Summoning gods of destruction had become a usual morning's work, I guessed. She calmly served refreshments while embroiling me in forces I had only read about — let alone understood or believed in. I wanted to broker a truce. I wanted some good news for Mo but couldn't find a way through. In fact, I was getting nowhere quickly.

"Mo's clinging on best he can, Ma'am. He respects you. But you'll lose him if you keep preaching the 'old' ways. Is there a half-way station here? Can you compromise?"

"Not when he cursed by DALCO. I'm gon' remove it. That's all. Ain't nothing but my callin'," she said with an upward inflection. This was line of argument hard to follow or dispute.

"All right, well…"

"Tell me, Clark, you getting enough wild love up there? Yo find something you like at last? A livin' breathin' girl to play god with?"

I was angered by that. This was too much.

"I love a woman," I said. "I know that. Plain and decent. There's nothing ill-bred in our love."

"You think months of wild love tells yo summin' about a woman, Clark? Think sex explains the soul of the body we want? No, sir. Loa whisper to you, but you don't make ears. You look, but yo won't find the force that drives a mother's love. Nor anything precious with yo cut and grab machines. Anyways, what yo do find yo dissolve in yo digesting tanks. An' all you get is a liquor, gud for nothing! Yo slow digestion of God's earth disgusts me!" Then she lifted her chin and took a breath.

"What right have you men to come here an' do that?"

"Every right!" I shouted angrily. "A man's right! What the hell right do you think? I've nothing else in mind than earning my keep. Keeping Case and me fed. Earning a day's pay for a day's work."

I grabbed some ice from the jug and smoothed it over my face and neck and shook my head. The sun had moved round now and I was no longer sitting in the shade. She calmly refilled my mug with coconut water and passed me more watermelon. I felt queasy for no good reason. Maybe it was the heat. Perhaps it was the thought of the unripe ackee. I couldn't say. Mo's mother had a power I didn't like. A power to make an X-ray of my psyche, a power to expose parts of me, still hidden from myself.

"Thank you kindly," I said quietly, trying to calm myself. I bit deep into the watermelon. It was sweet and cold. The juice dribbled from my mouth. She got up again and brought out a lime from indoors and came back to the table. Cutting it in half, she squeezed the juice over the red melon.

"That mos' refreshin' I do believe."

I shared the juiced melon. We sat quiet for a short time. Apart from when we spoke it seemed a lovely way to spend a hot afternoon. A casual 'at home' in the gentile company of a grandmother. But I'd a marked feeling she'd eventually hex me and send me back to DALCO, soul-stabbed and sick at heart. Mambos can spread evil as well as lift it. But how could I argue with a woman who'd spent her life spinning curses, summoning gods and stirring the book of Revelations like a bucket of cockroaches?

"Well, you got a piece to say, Clark? Say it."

"I've tried to. I don't like the way you're spoiling things for Mo. That's all."

"My, you on a mercy mission today. That it? Come here for purgation? What you can't purify, you burn up."

"Mo's a good man. C'mon — you want to control his life. We all have to get by. Some of us find unholy ways — others take a day's pay. Mo's not under any spell at the mine. He's not cursed or anyways different to other men; men who want the best for their families. Give him a chance. He's torn between your respect and his freedom."

"That right?"

"At least believe Mo's life needs to be lived, not railroaded. Will you do that for me? What you're doing to him now is not right or fair."

"'Yo got summin' right or fair to tell him?" She slammed her hand down on the table, making the crockery jump. "Mo tells me you a good man, Clark. Know that? But I think you all twisted up inside. A man who makes a mess of all he touches. Bribes his way to God and knows no heavenly shame at his doing." That sounded like a litany to me, an odd mixture of Christian humility and old Ethiopian mystique. But I knew it was something so deeply ingrained in these people it could never be shifted.

Mo's mother settled back in her chair and crossed herself. Then she took up a long cane to rest her hands on and spoke quietly.

"Show me yo hands. Don't be afraid, boy. I ain't gonna cut 'em off."

I held out my hands for her. Shadows from my fingers criss-crossed the red fruit.

"Palms up, Clark! Hold 'em out flat. That's it. Now, how long you been hard scrubbing them? Hmm? They all ugly and raw.

See? That because yo can't wash de murder blood off!" She traced the angled lines and roughened patches of skin.

"I saw the stain, moment you turned up. Yo marked by God. Did you scrub until the flesh glowed pink, then red, until maybe it broke open — and then some? What yo done here, mark yo for life."

I looked over at Falco – could he understand her? He seemed to be nodding. I looked at my hands again — scratched, swollen, red still.

"It's just mud stain, lady," I said. "Iron-rich mud stain." She pulled a lotion bottle out of her dress pocket. "You put that on it, boy. Might help drive it out." I was surprised at the kindness after her wild accusations and unpredictable temperament.

"All right."

"Yo steeped in yo own dark magic, Clark. Yo own flashfire and clouds. Yo wander lost in it like a moth wid no flame to rush to. Yo got summin' in yo more poisonous than anything we ever dreamed up. Daily yo leave our God-given earth shorn. Moving higher and higher up St. Katherine's mount, until yo done wringing every last drop of blood ore out of her.

She poured out the last of the drink. The melon was about finished too. I shook my head in disapproval and stood up. She looked up at me with a grim smile. "Go, while the lord givin' yo breath to live."

I got up, sighed — a little with relief — and walked back through the house. Falco nosed his way past me to the gate. The sun was still high and hot when I started my long walk back down to the bus stop.

Chapter 6

Blood Lake

We were standing outside the workers' canteen, at the pin board reading the roster. I slapped Mike on the back. "Says we got four weeks to complete, big man. The cuttings need to be finished by then. Seems like we're going back to work this Monday."

"Yeah, tink so too. Heard Krebbs going on about the relief crew. Ya hear? They plain near dead. Worked a fourteen-hour shift for six days. Then put in a whole weekend, makin' a five-week month."

"Tough for any man, even without the toxic air," I said. "Don't mention it to Case. About the only thing we bicker about is work and sloth. The two opposites of life. We are fine on love and fun. Remember Sansano? He told me there might be trouble here. Tried to warn me about the ridge. Case would fly at me if she thought the job required danger money."

Krebbs had crept up behind us while we were facing the board.

"You fellas cummin' to Magrite tonight?" He said. I guess he'd been standing behind us, listening. He leered over my shoulder.

"Get off me, Krebbs."

"What's that about danger money, boys?"

"Nothing to you."

"All right then. Fine night of dancing to be done at Magrite's afore we hit the dozers Monday." He shimmied on the spot. I laughed at him.

"Mike mentioned you saw the relief crew, near worked to death?"

"Yep. And it ain't gonna get any better. So, you lads better be ready for some real work. We're going higher, and that's a fact."

Mike and I walked away, keeping our thoughts to ourselves for a while. We headed down towards the blue-painted settling tanks where the ore was steeped in hot caustic soda. "Krebbs gives me the creeps. He one of the worst fuckers here."

"Forget him. You do yourself harm thinking like dat."

I nodded and placed my palms on the side of the warm tank. "Here is where raw earth is 'digested', as Mo's mother put it." The tanks were nearly sixty feet high. Mike walked into the shade. "So what you wanna tell me, Clark?"

We'd stopped in the laddered shadows. His face loomed over me in darkened stripes. "Sounds like the holiday is well and truly over. You fancy staying on? Or shall we all git – as you folks say."

"I dunno. Got nuttin' else to do."

I looked into his eyes. "Me neither."

For some of us the mine was a forgotten layer in life, a dry limbo we'd crawled into to escape our origins. Until I met Case, I'd needed an in-between world. A place to cut adrift, in a line of work I never imagined doing. I'd hoped to just lie on that raft, in the open ocean, staring up at the sky and birds without a damn qualm, needing only currents and the shifting tides to bring opportunities for my rescue. My contract was for a year, but I renewed it soon after I fell for Case. They had a stiff policy against men shacking with women on camp, but we all went off and got old Pattern II tribal marriage blessings, 'our Jamaican way,' going back to the days of polygamy law. We satisfied the local landowners we meant business. We qualified being limited to just one wife outside the church. You needed money to join the church way back then.

The warmer weather burned away our germs and freed us to carry on 'kissing', much as we had before. Only now, with the germs all burned up and no colds or fevers to distract us, we slept with the sheets off again and my fevered sweating slowed.

Numerous ailments subsided with it. Case's asthma improved and with the Mambo's lotion, my hands lost some of their redness. Mo brought more phials of the stuff to the hut whenever it ran out. Truth to tell as the months passed over and my early shifts began, I often lay back and thought of my days in Winchester, comparing them to Jamaica.

In England, the sharp morning air was a thing I'd grown accustomed to. On the downs it blew in on a mist some days and broke the dawn quiet. The smell of it hurt the inside of your nose— a sudden, flint-sharp coldness that pricked the senses. After the early mist dissolved, the sun took the frost out of the ground and thin skeins of fog rose up and clung to the grass and tree roots to swirl for an hour round your feet, never rising above waist height, until it, too, dispersed in the morning sunshine. An hour after dawn the thickets and hedgerows would fill with birdsong. Walking through patches of forest, I remember the sight of the bluebells adorned in dappled sunlight. On those clear mornings my early walks through Chilcomb, near old St Andrews, gave me a new sense of wonder. I'd longed for adventures further afield than those chalk downs, but now, on our morning drives to the blood lakes, riding shotgun on the old wagon, as Buck called it, there was not the sense of adventure. The striking colour of the processed ore left us always with a sense of self-disgust.

Buck Jackson took Mike and me up to the bauxite lakes at least once a month. It was an arduous drive, fraught with pot-holes, boggy lanes and overgrown turns, and we often got stuck. When we finally climbed sleepily down from the warm cabin, a leaden coldness seeped from the ground. It entered our feet and noses objectionably. The damp came through my clothes and my rubber boots and was very uncomfortable. There was a sour smell to the air here, like no other. No birds in the trees and the sense of limbo that gave to the forest brought on a strange feeling in me.

As we drew nearer to the edge of the lake - the place the field manuals called a residual disposal area - the red earth fanned out wide and thick. Against its perimeter ran a thick line of trees. Jacarandas and limes, elms and all-spice were the dominant species. The leaves of the inner trees were prematurely yellow. In the middle distance, great pools of rust-red water had formed. It was too dangerous to walk out to them. As usual, Mike set up the theodolite and we took various measurements from poles spaced at regular intervals around the shoreline. Iron oxide, silicon oxide and calcium oxide sit heavily dispersed in these muds, packed with sodium oxide and titanium dioxide. Before we returned to camp, Buck would need about a dozen core samples, so we'd hammer in the tubes to a depth of about four metres. After we'd loaded the tubes, we'd stop for a smoke on the truck. It was hard to stop the earth from staining your cigarettes and when it did, it looked horribly like lipstick smears. I knew it was critical to detect that no minerals had leeched into the groundwater system. The whole rack of substances in these muds was highly poisonous and the local community would be at risk if the groundwater was fouled. Late afternoon we drove back, mainly in silence, though Buck was always the most cheerful of us. He didn't seem to mind the mud lakes, or the coring. His was a well-paid job, and that fact was the only thing he kept front of mind.

Chapter 7

Magrite's

At Magrite's, we drank pot-stilled rum, Appleton's, or Blackwell's, if I could lay my hands on them. Blackwell's was the rum I liked best of all. I kept a bottle of it in the cabin and treated myself to a nip after work. Better still, I liked it when all six of us snaked down the path to town together to sit outside the little cafés or late-night bars crowding the hills around Morgan's Bluff. Our company of red monks — hard-living, yet full of adventure and romance — ate, slept, drank, lived and worked together. Some days it felt like there was nothing we could not do or accomplish if we put all our heads and hearts together. Love, in all its passion and heartache, threaded through us in those times, like a nascent tapestry, symbol-rich, with hope's silvered edge outlining our characters. Today I carried my aluminum hip flask and stole a nip as we walked. Sometimes, the girls brought a thermos of coffee and I'd offer up 'brown milk' for Mike and me. Mo rarely drank and when he did, it was certainly a laughing matter. Fortunately, we had enough diversity among us to argue about anything and everything. Today was no different. Mike fancied stopping by the old lookout on the far side of the bluff. The girls felt it was too far – this was a night out and they'd made an effort to look their best.

Even I shaved carefully that morning, using one of the new Gillettes Case bought me. Smooth-faced, I looked a mite younger — strange how a razor blunts the scythe of time. Case had worked hard to coerce me to go to the Abyssinian's gig. So, on that last evening at 7pm, we walked into town with Anne, Mike and Juanita. The first mile was a rough path through the bush —

uphill mostly. The path was a shortcut on the map which avoided the circuitous road that ran inland before swinging back to the coastal shanties. We ploughed on that night, having had a little more to drink to begin with than usual. My shirt was stuck to me uncomfortably and I could have done with just stopping on the bluff and not bothering with Magrite's. Maybe even sleeping out tonight. It was a long time since I'd slept under the stars with Case, but still, steadying our breath and watching where we stepped, our band of bauxite red monks continued their pilgrimage. At the brow of the hill we paused on the wide tarmac road. During the day, this was full of mining traffic — the biggest of the loaders hurtled along here like thunder, alongside dilapidated buses for workers cropping out of the parish. We took the short leg of the road this evening which crossed onto the bush path at St. Katherine's Point. I put my arm around Case as she looked cold in the moonlight.

In jungle again, with the fresh green canopy blowing above our heads, and the frogs and crickets keeping up their usual throaty trill and tingle, our voices were joined occasionally by a snoring tree frog. I pitied the lone male calling from his hollow bark tree.

"Don't you guys think we've sightseen enough? I'm getting cold now and Case is already cold."

"There's always one – or two fun suckers!" Mike said.

"We are not fun suckers – just cold suckers!" Case giggled. Mike tutted loudly.

"I'm a cold sucker too, Case," Anne complained. She came by and snuggled into us both."

"Alright, alright – I will tear myself away from the most beautiful moonlit night of my life. I've never seen the sea so calm and the sky so clear."

Mike drew his bulk towards Anne and slapped me on the back. "Magrite's everybody. Forward ho!"

Though I say it myself, I'd made a decent effort to spruce up tonight and by both sweating and freezing alternately the temperature was hardly helping my cred.

"That's a good stride you got there, Clark!"

I ignored Case. But I was striding along in a strong pair of riveted Levi 901s and a pressed tartan checked shirt. I was rather happy in myself. I'd bought a heavy pair of boots recently, in good, smooth, supple leather, from a reputable maker in Kingston. He'd told me that he'd made shoes for Sean Connery and still had the lasts to prove it.

Mike tilted his Panama hat back on his head. "Clark, you got those ounces you owe me, man? I bin keepin' on about them for some days. I'm wonderin' why you haven't paid me up yet? You can't have forgot. I never let you."

I pointed to a large moth, almost the size of my hand. The wide grey-blue wings were spread across some tree bark to dry.

"You do keep reminding me, Mike – but I forgot why I owe you. Why do I owe you ounces, Mike?"

Mike Jakarta laughed in a short wheeze. "On account of that kale, carrot and potato chowder I made you an' Case. That's why, sweetheart."

I remembered the thick chowder. It was very good, but it wasn't worth ounces. In fact, not even one ounce.

"I do have an ounce, Mike. Without the 's'. And it could be yours when we get to Magrite's."

"I'll take an ounce as a lay down – yo' can be sure of that. Rest you better come up with priddy soon."

I slapped his shoulder. "Oh, I'm sure. I'm sure as grass is weed, that all I've got is an ounce for you."

Mike tilted his hat forward and shook his head. The panama was composed of a finely threaded weave; expensive. Master weavers of the true *super finos* are in short supply nowadays. He walked beside me now with his Partagas Corona stub protruding from his mouth. "I'm listening, and I'm keepin' score, Clark."

He spoke as if to say the debt was trivial to him in size, but big in principle. When Mike smoked and talked at the same time, he spoke only from the left side of his face, hardly ever removing his cigar. But the facial contortion suited him. I knew if I tried it, I'd look like a cartoon gangster. Mike's father had worked at the

Partagas factory when he was young, and now Mike rarely smoked another brand of cigars. But for all his patriarchal loyalty he was a bad smoker — a short puffer, who gave no time for the ember to cool and give rise to the delicate shades of flavour that such cigars offer a real smoker. He seemed to revel more in the great coils of blue smoke that hid his big face now. In the twilight, the setting sun behind us had bruised the clouds mauve and red-pink. You might see nicer countryside or get nicer jobs, I'm sure — swim nicer beaches even — but you'd never meet nicer people than this crew. I admit, I loved them to bits.

"You okay, Clark?"

"Sure, Mike. Why ask?"

"You gone quiet. Everything okay with Case? You did wanna come out?"

"Listen — only two more Case and Clark questions all evening. That's your quota OK?"

"Then answer my third."

"I wanted to come. After I wrote a little today I felt like a change of scene. I saw something odd today – don't ask me what exactly. And there was just a feeling about it, a something. I don't know what."

"What was it?"

"Krebbs showed me a rag doll he found in his excavator. Something like a child's toy. But unchildlike in many ways."

"Inside the grabber?"

"Yep. He flung it away. Said it was filled with writing and a bird claw, of all things!"

"I see. Well, 'maybe this is a good time for a drink? Been a long four weeks without much beer, hasn't it?"

He puffed at me again and this time the smoke stung my eyes. "Just you keep that damn smoke out of my face," I said.

He switched sides around me.

"Anyways, Clark, lots happening on the ridge. I saw Kolo today. As far up on the mount as I've seen a crewman climb; birds circling his head. He waved down at me. I pointed to the birds, flocking above him, the black shapes worrying his soul. He hollered something back, but I couldn't make it out."

"I saw him up there too – but I couldn't make out if it really was Kolo. That's one hell of a climb … not to mention getting back down!"

"If he got that far, the ol' goat, he get down all right. But whatcha think he lookin' for?"

"I've no idea. He's always hanging out with the site geologist."

"Frank Gran… Grangie?"

"Granger." I looked at Mike. Mike was smiling at sixty degrees North West, his upturned lips snagging the cigar hard.

"Thass him, Granger. What you think they saw?"

"A big mess, probably. Seams overworked and nowhere else to cut. Unless you tackled the upper deposits – them thin, mean gulches. Only the bluff untouched. See long ways from the ridge!"

"Yes, out west to the red lakes near the mountains, brimful of sludge. And east across the Caribbean,"

"Those lakes at the foot of some dangerous slopes, full of rain-cut gullies."

I continued. "And north — out to the brighter rims of the surrounding hills where the air's colder and the mists of rain hang low even in January. Then down to where we'll start the new deposits, which I spoke to Stuart about last week."

"Yeah?"

"He's on our side. Says Krebbs is right. Looks like we are going higher and it will be tough." I saw Case turn as she overheard our conversation. She'd been looking intently at a praying mantis clinging to the underside of a big palm leaf.

"Clark, leave work at work – I don't want to hear 'bout the mine all night. Time off is time freed!"

Mike smiled. "We need to cut a new terrace to get the dozers in, Clark. Those slopes' are pretty tricky. Am in no shape for danger money. Not after this summer."

"Me neither."

Mike looked apprehensively at me. He'd been at DALCO a year longer than I had. His eyes turned cold. "This mount got deep caves and springs, Clark. Mebbe all kind of hazards inside her."

"Then I'll ask Krebbs about a guarantee and time off between site inspections. I want—" He stopped me.

"Shh now, they could finish you up for that kinda talk. Man, yo get yer cards in a flash here. Must never make demands, obligations, nuttin' like that. And don't turn nuttin' down neither. With danger money, always say you consider it. Wait for de others to jump in. Promise me, Clark? Else we be history in the blink of an eye."

"Mike, I've got no inclination to die early; we've got to stand up to them – else we'll be less than history."

Case came up level with us. "Who's dying early?"

"No-one," I said. She put her arm around my waist, and I went quiet.

Mike dropped back to let Case have her way. He waited back to walk with Anne. I heard her Texan voice cut through the zing of the crickets.

"You talking work and money again, Mike? All I care for is a drink; like Case, I just want to dance and taste the spice of life, hun!"

Case shouted out to her. "Oh! Tonight, we gonna party like it's our last on God's earth, Anne." Mike smiled, wrapped his big paws around her slim waist and hugged her close.

Anne wore an ivory dress and pink block heels, making her seem even taller than the usually bespectacled, prim and carefully spoken girl who kept the back office under her thumb. Tonight, she had relaxed her look. She had tied a long red shawl round her body, to avoid marking her dress on the walk. I knew Anne could be overbearing at times, over-manicured and rather temperamental; but she looked after Mike very well. Tonight, her dress was just low cut enough to hint at finer pleasures, but they were not the luxury furnishings God gave to some. Juanita came alongside me and Case. She seemed especially quiet.

"Mo okay?" Case asked.

"Yea, he's fine. This is such a lovely time to walk, to feel the soft evening breeze."

Anne smiled. "Well, honey, you enjoy. Don't let us bother you none!"

"Oh, you no bother. It's just that I feel like dancing and being quiet and cosy at the same time."

I liked that. Juanita often said things I liked.

"I'd find that hard to do, Juan, but not to think about," I said. She had styled her hair this evening into a sixties look with a deep curl at the front; it reminded me of the Motown Supremes.

"Juanita, you look finer than a sunset if I may say? Ol' Mo's missin' de fun tonight."

Mike wheezed, puffing away while hugging Anne close. I lost sight of them suddenly, guessing they'd dropped back to 'seize the day' or something better. To the rest of us, Anne and Mike had always looked inseparable. Case felt they were destined for each other. But neither of them believed that; neither of them felt their love was written in the stars. We'd talked a lot about relationships in the hut, and sometimes we hit on the downturns and the weary bitterness that creeps in when you lose respect for what you have. Other times we hit the heights, with that sense of wonder and beauty which possesses the mundane and the plentiful. It was hard to avoid clichés about love, or betrayal, or the dozens of other dams which inhibit the force of true love. Mo related his non-stop dizzying ride with Juanita, which propels the mind at lightspeed, and how that time spent apart causes a hollow ache which is hardly ever mended. When you meet again, and the sudden chills that a single, piercing look can bring to shake the heart, you touch on the metaphysical; the joining of souls. I suppose there is something in that. For different couples, love acts and repays them differently, but the constant is to believe always, to cherish whatever purity of love you have found; to not treat the essence of human compatibility with disdain. Often, Mike mesmerised me by the way he put it all down to luck — luck that they met in the first place, and lucky that both of them saw the simple chance they could take for happiness.

For Mike there was nothing much to relate or dedicate to poetics through the ages – the love they had was just love: equal, balanced and alive. They were just people in love with love. Case and I were a little different – we had wider issues, details that were still shadowed and unresolved. I felt that under scrutiny in those circles of talk, our love stood in a less pure light, but some love is not on a wide plain — it is on a ledge, and perhaps at times, all of life is on a ledge. I told Mike that if the fact of true love is unbelieved and so too the notion of love at first sight, then fate should have no reputation – nor should sexual magnetism exist, or even that plunge into foolery, where the feet are no longer on the ground. Love has many facets – some know only the burning want, others simply the wonder and some, sadly, only an indelible pain . . .

Now the two of them appeared not only closer but attuned to each other in a remarkable way – possibly more so after Mike's accident. The previous autumn, the big man had torn his arm up, sliced clean through muscles and arteries. Hospitalised in Kingston for a week, he was ordered to rest and put down the 'damn' cigars. It took nearly forty stitches to sew his bicep back together. Anne had nursed him, cooked, washed, cleaned and fetched him new boxes of cigars from Kingston for two months. Mike called her his 'Pattern Wife'. She also gave him quaco bush leaves to chew on. I'd lunched with them both around that time and I enjoyed hearing her laugh: a clear, long-toned exaltation. Anne always brightened after a few drinks and regaled us with tales of her too-cutesy childhood in Texas. I was looking forward to tonight now and having the best of times.

"Hey, dreamer! What were you and Mike talking about?" asked Case.

"Just work. Nothing to worry about."

"As long as you mean that."

"I do mean it! Saying that, I wonder if we were meant for each other."

"All right — don't get smart."

"You're saying we aren't meant then – just loaned?"

"Well I like a loaned soul. Drives me."

"What else could my soul be?"

"Owned. And I wouldn't like that. It would prove too high-maintenance."

"Do you always understand what you say?"

"Yes — because I listen."

Beneath us the town stretched out into an untidy collection of shanty huts with bigger homes dotted among the fields. Its scant lights formed shimmering yellow globes in the darkness. Here and there the telegraph lines sagged low, touching the roofs almost. They looked as slack as we *Doubloons* did on hot days. We continued down the slope and reached Mack's Garage: just two rusted pumps and a shelter resembling a guard house. He nodded us by. Another lane turned past the disused pig sheds and finally we cut the corner to Magrite's. Here the bar was open; a brazier burned high, and through in the open yard a good crowd was jostling for space. When you hit Magrite's you take her as you find her. There is nothing to rile against. However makeshift, disorganized, grubby or hellishly hot you find her — Magrite's is home from home. You bought your drinks from the small wood and corrugated iron cabin on the left, then moved to the log seats. I got to the front line and called for a beer. A tall Negro with a gravel voice, Kurt Jecker, otherwise known as Jex, ran the bar. He caught my eye and nodded. Jex kept things sweet here, cultivating night-scented jasmine, which suited him and the place; the intoxicating, nocturnal plant and the crowds who came; his night moths, to pollinate in the warm air. Here folk settled on hot rhythms and soul-born reggae. There was rarely any trouble at Magrite's.

The bar was named after Jex's elderly mother, Margaret, and when or if it came to fights, Jex was always fair. Just as Margaret was, or so he told us. He rarely called the police unless he feared the place would get broken up. Jex hated the sight of violence, but he could turn mean if he had to. I heard he broke a man's arm once. Onlookers stepped away as the bone broke through the skin and blood spurted over their shirts. Such tales in the parish pass into folklore easily.

Case came up and took my beer off the bar. "Having fun? Dreamer! You're meant to be buying a round, not schmoozing alone."

"Coming up."

"I know what's planned, Clark." Case put her arm around my waist. "You're brooding on it. They're moving higher up the ridge. To thinner workings. Does it worry you?"

"Not much."

"Truthfully. It's me you're talking to now, not the boys."

"Just needs care and hard work. Strong terracing. And then we've got to put it all back as we found it."

"It's a sheer slope. Why?"

"I'm not saying that. I mean – it's going to be tough, that's all."

"You're thinking danger money?"

"Maybe not, just hard work."

"Isn't it always at DALCO?" said Anne, bursting in. "Clark, where's my drink?"

"Coming."

I sent the girls back to Mike to pick our seats. Jex pushed through the crowd and came up to me.

"Hey, Clark, I put a stack of old chairs in the corner. Help yo self."

He shook my hand firmly, smiling. "If you guys in tonight, no trouble, ya hear?" The deep voice ground over his verbs like stone on corn. I nodded. He was joking of course. We never caused any trouble. I put three Red Stripes and two double Appleton's on a tray. On a log table nearby there was a large block of ice wrapped in a towel with a pick next to it. If you wanted ice, you cut your own. Reggae was blaring from an old ghetto blaster. The tape decks were fixed shut with green gaffer tape.

"Jex!" I called, startling him, while he was tickling a local girl. "No sign of the tribute band yet? Gone eight thirty!" He sauntered over.

"Don't worry Clark – cool down. 'Ave a drink. They be here soon. Let the moon come up. Let de feelings grow inside." He looked me up and down. "Hell An' I got some stinger repellant if you white folks wants it?"

I ducked to the right and gave him a playful body blow.

"No, we white folks are tougher than your mosquitoes now."

The evening shoved on, and around eleven the band pitched up in an old pick-up truck. They'd driven most of the way with a flat tyre and no spare.

"Jeez, where you guys bin?" Jex shouted. "I got a big crowd in. Bin drinkin' all night. Dem halla. You don' show? What's the deal?"

The driver got out and slammed the door of the cab.

"MAN! Yuh got no respeck, Jex! Got a flat down at de bay. We struggle to make it up here."

Jex pulled at his knitted slouchie and bit his lip. "Ya no gud," he whined. "Bin hour too long!"

Carew, the drummer, hustled in and spoke for the others.

"Dat some climb to this shit hole, Jecker! Me met you lass week. Yo say was noting. It easy route to de ridge. Dat ain't so. Don't go blamin' us gang."

He ambled to the rear of the truck and unbolted the tailgate. They manhandled a battered bass drum down into the road. A short Negro inspected the claw hooks.

"Watch me hoop, dat cost dear!"

Then they stood around moping for a few minutes, looking daggers at each other and Jecker.

"Okay. Okay," Jex said at last. "Me leggo dis time."

He patted their backs and helped them off the wagon with the rest of the gear. "C'mon now! Jess git set-up and play yuhs hearts out. Me big crowd in to see yo bad guys. Be fiddy or more out back."

As we waited, we chatted about the real Abyssinians, wondering what had happened to them, until Anne asked me if I knew that Mo had gone into town earlier. I told her I didn't, but I wondered why.

"He never said anything to me. What did he want?"

Case took a pull from her can. "I thought we'd got everything we need. Mike and I shopped this morning."

Anne spoke in hushed tones. "Mo wasn't shopping. He's gone to the balm yard. After a blessin', he will take a series of baths. It's a local custom, a cure for illness or something."

I felt startled by the news. The baths sounded ominous. I knew he'd been sick and I knew Juanita was worried.

"She told me his mother's been writing to him almost every day. I think he feels he's let her down." Case had suspected something like this might happen.

"Remember when I went up to see the Mambo?" I said to her. "I told you it was like meeting a hellcat. I spoke up for Mo best I could. But I don't think it did any good. She was Obeah, or Mambo – or something else. I hardly knew what to say. She knew more about the mine than I expected. Mo must report back to her like a missionary in a whore house."

"Well, maybe a few baths will restore him," Case said cheerfully.

"Those balm yards are all hocus pocus, Case," hissed Anne. "I think he needs the camp doctor."

I looked sharply at Anne but said nothing. Mike laid his hand on top of hers. We left it at that. Case nudged me. She pointed to the fray in the yard.

"Let's get this party started, baby! Are you *on* the 'Case' tonight?"

"I'm always *on* the Case. But I'll dance later." She waved a mock goodbye and filtered into the crowds.

"Have another, Mike?" I asked.

"Sure, rum, but I gotta dance." I took our glasses and the tray and walked back to the cabin. Behind the table with the ice block, Jex was pulling wires about, switching a thousand plugs into mini adapters.

"Don't burn us down tonight, Jex!" He snatched up the ice pick and shooed me away.

I accidently bumped into Krebbs. "Hey, where you all sittin?" he asked me. I tilted my head forward. He nodded.

"Oak's, be over later. Got Barbara here. She's pukin' already."

"Christ!" I said, but I wasn't surprised. They both drank the day through, Monday to Sunday.

"Later, man," I said quietly. "Oh, Krebbs, you did fling that thing out, yeah?"

"Yeah – it's gone man – gone into the earth."

When I got back from the bar, Mike and Case were still dancing. The yard was jammed with rolling bodies now. I plonked down the reed tray full of drinks and handed out beers to Anne and Juanita. The band had struck up fiercely, going into a firm favorite, *Satta Massagana*. We all cheered and forgiveness fanned out as free as moonlight. Everyone got to their feet. After that number, the skank kicked in harder and louder and like a perfect spliff, unveiled white-toothed smiles. I sat back down, a little out of breath, in order to relax with Anne and Juanita. I was never into grass and hated the sickly smell of it.

Anne was sitting cross-legged on the bench, in full flow. "So his family bad to you too?" she remarked. "I know they're hard on him. But you're such a sweet girl. What you done to deserve that?"

To me, she sounded set on extracting information. I watched Juanita as she thoughtfully scratched Mo's name in the condensation on her beer can.

"They fine to me really. I'm okay. Mo gets uptight about his mother."

"Clark says he's terrified of her. Stays off work when she gets at him. Mo has such a kind way. Always nice to me. Never a bad word 'bout no one."

"Yes. We so glad Clark asked us to share. Mo is very fond of you, Clark." She leaned forward to look me in the eye. "He tells you everything."

"Good ol Mo. He'll pull through," I said. "Jesus, look at Mike. If the big fella tumbles, somebody's gonna die!" Mike was thrashing about dancing — if you could call it that — looking like he was sleeping through a nightmare, still smoking his cigar.

"God, I've had too much beer already." Anne blew out her cheeks and pushed the can away. She rubbed her stomach. "Far too gassy. How about a whisky?"

I looked at the tray. Mike's double Appleton was sitting there warming. "Here, take Mike's," I said. "I'll get him another." Anne clinked Mike's glass against mine.

"A toast then. To the six doubloons!"

"To the six doubloons!" We shouted, I drank up and stared into the crowd. The band looked as if they were floating above the bobbing heads. Jex was hovering side of stage, lip-syncing with a mic.

"That is so fine," Anne said. "Such a nice, warm, fuzzy feeling at last." She turned to Juanita.

"Seeing you there in that light, honey, how I do like your dress. It's the one you wore to the last dance, ain't it? Suits you just so. Ivory white. Smooth on those nice curves, with all them tiny embroidered flowers. So pretty. Men here delight in curvy gals." Anne brushed her hands over her own skirt quickly, tugging at the creases. Juanita pulled her shoulders back.

"It makes me look royal, Mo says. I like to wear it on the hottest of days. It's pure cotton, sea island cotton." Anne tipped her head back and finished the double.

"Sounds expensive."

"I don't afford much," Juanita said. I frowned at Anne and smiled at Juanita.

"Mo bought it for you?" I asked.

"Last year," she replied. I was about to change the subject, but Anne trumped me.

"How are you and him getting along, honey? I don't hear a thing, you folks being prone to nights up at Dale. And all those weekends away, you sneaky lil' angels."

"Oh, we fine."
Anne made a long face.

"No, really we are," Juanita whispered, sipping her beer.

"Look at me a moment, darling. You got such a sweet curl on your fringe today." Anne looked down at her empty glass. Juanita smiled back.

"Just tongs, all natural. I don't fuss with it."

"Oh, I do natural — everybody does natural," carped Anne. "I say, it's truly a blessing for Mo to be with such a nice simple girl. Mike says your personality reminds him of shortcake, hot tea and butterscotch. Clark! – see here. Mike has had a perfect jewel of a ring, made for me from Gibbsite, I believe. Here, look."

"Well, I suppose you think it very fine. Quite the wonder?"

"Yes I do."

"Well, Gibbsite is one of the most *common* of all minerals. You can find it anywhere, even if Mike did find that one. I could find another like it in a second."

"Well, it won't be this one, will it? This one here is unique in the fact." Anne turned away from me now. "Juanita you were telling *me* about Mo?"

"At weekends we go into the mountains, where Mo's cousin lives. It's much cooler there. The sky is so clear and beautiful in the evening. We sit out and watch the clouds and the birds – the kling klings. They make so much noise. More than Mo. Up there the coffee grows so green and fresh. The family have a get-together on Sunday afternoons, everyone eating, drinking, talking their week up. Then we walk into the pines at five, through the firebreaks and just stroll and breathe clean mountain air." I looked at Juanita, her dress shining in the low light, her brown skin silky smooth, her eyes sparkling, flitting around over the crowd.

"Sounds a pretty place," Anne said, tugging at her skirt again. "I like a cool evening breeze too."

"Well, some nights it turns cold and we go inside to lie down by the fire. Mo snuggles up to me like a little boy. We sit in the glow and plan our lives and he tells me about all the places he's going to take me to. We going all the way to England someday. Gonna pick flowers in them London parks and go in a black taxicab."

I sat back. "Sounds idyllic, Juanita."

The reggae had relaxed to a softened throb. Case was still dancing, pulling sultry moves that excited. I looked further into the smouldering dark. The crowds were a live mass of black shapes, rhythmically melding, flowing, folding into the music. The tribute band strayed into an old Marley classic, *No Woman, No Cry*. Mike was grinning from ear to ear, Case's sinuous, pulsing outline gripping his attention. Anne snatched up her beer can again. "So, Mo has a cousin?" She said tartly, waking me from my erotic adventures.

"I believe Jan works on Morgan's plantation. They sell into a co-operative."

"All the *little* plantations do," said Juanita. "When I say little, I mean under five hundred acres."

"I know you don't mean a backyard, honey, but in Texas that's a front lawn. Oh, my! All this red dust on my skirt. I can't wear anything white myself. Takes but two minutes and it's smirched. How does one keep a dress so pure?"

"I keep my hands off it."

I nudged Anne. "You look well, Anne. You've caught the sun at last. Job kept you pale."

"I don't like too much sun, Clark. I go red, then itch, then yellow. So I keep a wide brim for sunny days." She had shut me out before. Now I felt like I was being dismissed.

"Did Mike see his pa when he came to the gate last month?" asked Juanita, pointedly.

"No. And please don't tell him. Poor Mike was on the infill when he came. All that moaning and shouting. I rushed to the fence and gave him some money. He took it quick enough. But I don't want Mike to know. None of the men here know. Case knows. Please make it our secret?"

"Don't you share family troubles?"

"It's not that."

"What is it?"

"Oh, now don't get me started. There are things I've had to put behind me. Let's not wake the dead tonight."

"What sort of things? Has somebody passed? What do you mean?"

"Well, my little sister lost her baby. And I haven't been able to bring myself to write to her. Life goes on. What can I say? We all go on and we've got to be happy – to live the life we got. I mean, what difference do awkward sentiments make anyway? Any upset forces me to think back when life likes to go on – or should."

"Oh, I don't know, sometimes we —"

"I have no gift for words – for saying the right thing. I'm plain and simple about things – mostly." Juanita looked at her lovingly.

"Just be sure she's all right. I'm sure she will be. But you should inquire. I'll say a little prayer for the lost one tonight, if you don't mind? I'll pray that your sister be well, get back on her feet soon." I continued listening to them but stopped myself from making idle comments.

"That's good and kind of you, Juanita. I suppose getting herself back to work will be a hard thing. They gave her such a maternity send-off. Thirty-three weeks gone she was when a bus ran up onto the pavement when she was at the station early one morning. Driver half asleep. Bus clipped her and she went down hard on the kerbstone; bleeding bad. By the time they got her to hospital she'd miscarried. Our mother wrote me —" Anne paused.

"Don't think of it now – it's OK."

"I'm so sorry. I shouldn't burden you with it all. You so young and with so much love ahead of you."

"It's all right. Let me help. Trust the Lord. He forgives our sins."

Anne stiffened. "Why, there ain't nothing to forgive. Ain't no sin. Was that driver, that's all."

"Is she married?"

"Well, no, but look —"

"God forgive. Maybe she marry soon. Make it right."

"An innocent has died, girl! Oh please, let's not fall out tonight. I need a drink this evening — not a priest. What with all this talk of danger money and Mike working high up on the ridge."

Anne stopped talking. I'd heard enough now. I thought about racing to the bar for more whisky but held back. Her story did get me wondering though, I mean on just how hard a task was ahead of us all. If Sansano had thought the ridge a tough play, that was a pretty good sweat-gauge to me.

"I'm sorry, Annie. It's just our way. Folks find it hard to understand." Juanita put her arm around her. Anne picked herself up a little.

"Well, for us it just sounds all mixed up – that's all, that kind of talk, 'bout marriage and sin and the like. Reminds of a christening when the little mite was said to have been born in sin – and it just only a few months old. Don't know-one respect innocence no more? Well, no harm done yet. I'm rather fractious about all kinds of things right now."

"I'll pray and light a candle. I'll light one tonight." Anne elbowed me and handed me her empty glass.

"Clark, will you be so kind as to get me another drink?" I picked up the tray and plunged back into the crowd. Afterwards the mood swung up again and I joined Case. We danced long into the night. But it was a far cry from the barbaric dancing and singing I'd done in Kingston's bars, with their rum toasts after each number, followed by banana dumplings and Surawa sauce.

Around three in the morning, Case grabbed hold of me for a final fling, 'Yim Mas Gan' (Praise the Lord). After that I knocked back one for the road, grabbed a chunk of ice and we started back to camp.

That last evening had proven a happy wake for our month off. The vacation had flown by. It seemed like only a moment had passed since I'd bathed with Case in the rock pool and we'd sat there watching the first sunsets of April. The bauxite mine had retooled now. Tomorrow the dozers would whirr and clatter again in the seams. These past weeks had seen a new road cleared toward the high ridge too; the one I'd seen Kolo climb. I thought about how rich agriculture had died in these parts when the mine opened, cutting open the old fields. The farmers had sold off their livelihoods for bauxite. The red mounds grew and the long barges came upriver to transport the ore back to West Peak or

Manchester. Old heavy barges drifted on the red-veined rivers now like slow cumbersome beasts, with their ogre-like bargemen, masked and wrapped head to toe in ruby cotton, gently raking their loads level in the morning mist.

We walked from Magrite's arm-in-arm. I smoothed ice over my face and neck. Then I handed the ball to Case, who dropped it while trying to tuck the thing down Mike's shirt.

"Case! Hey yo, juss behave, gal. You know you been bad all night long!"

"Who says?"

Juanita followed on behind. Mike walked away and took hold of Anne. They strolled between us, until Case sat down unexpectedly in the middle of the path. Mike lifted her up into his big arms and swung her over his shoulder. She collapsed into laughter and cried to be put down.

"God, I can't breathe. Mike, you're squashing my guts!" Case wriggled like a fish, screaming and kicking her legs, but Mike had a firm hold. "Put me down, ya big lug! I'm gonna be sick."

"Then don' go sittin' in the road, Case. It dangerous. You mighta bin killed."

I caught up with Anne and I told her that I wanted a Texan lullaby at bedtime tonight. Or an old story of the Mississippi.

"I ain't never been to the Mississippi, Clark, you know that. My daddy was a Texas ranger. And he cap your ass for callin' me a southern belle." She drawled her reply to make me laugh. Then she gave us some more ridiculous excuses in southern tones. Seeing Case freed from Mike's capture I grabbed her back into my arms to keep her moving along.

"Wonder how Mo is?" I asked her.

"Fine. Think he'll be back tonight?"

"I hope so."

Juanita came up beside us. "I heard you. He'll be fine, I'm sure." Anne hitched her thin shoulder straps up again. I wondered why she wore those thin strappy tops, if all night she was going to pull them about in ad-hoc embarrassment. The mysteries of lingerie and dresses foxed me.

"I guess Mo's a lot cleaner than when we last see him," Mike said.

"Oh, don't make fun. He's a mixed-up boy," said Anne.

"With a Mambo mother," I cautioned. Juanita ignored us.

When we reached the old crossroads, Mike stepped forward and pointed west. "See the old lighthouse on the bluff of Morgan's Bay? Real pretty sight 'bout now." We moved between the trees until we had an unobstructed view, then we looked out. The lighthouse's grey stone walls had crumbled in the storms, but the tower still stood high, a proud forty feet. The moon was honeyed now and the grey stones shone pale amber against the dark sky.

"Guess they used to light beacons all along these cliffs," I said.

"Plenty tales of smugglers on this coast," said Mike.

The distant sea looked black from this height. A light wind ruffled the shallows, forming silver crests on the waves. At Morgan's Bay the variable tides ran quick, flooding or receding from the sandy crescents in minutes. If you were ignorant of the tide you could be cut off easily and swept onto the reef. Clouds blotted the moon suddenly, soaking up the light. I switched on my torch and pointed it back down the path.

"You had that all along?" cried Anne.

"Sure. I always carry it."

"Then use it, Clark. I've scraped my best shoes twice already."

We walked in silence a while. Everyone was tired. When we arrived at camp, we showed our passes at the gate and trawled back to the hut. The big floodlights were on. The place was lit up like a circus at night. I opened the big door and we all filed in. Our footsteps sounded louder in the dark. They echoed on the old boards, creaking and thumping as we entered. Mo was snoring from his back-end bunk. "Guess he's restored," I sniggered. Case shushed me.

"Let's get to bed now, sweetie," Anne whispered. She kissed Mike on the cheek and dragged him into their flop. I crashed onto the bed.

"I said shh, you'll wake Mo." Case slipped off her dress and climbed in. I felt her warm breasts press against my chest. I hugged her tight. With the cold bedsheets wrapped against our skin, we kissed goodnight.

Usually, we'd all stay up to watch the sun come over the bay from the canteen stoop. But like I said, we were bushed that night. The last thing I remember is the quiet. Not even the crickets were making a sound.

Chapter 8

Papa Legba

In the darkness, the hut shook terribly. It twisted sideways first — then the joints splintered. The galvanised stilts mooring the building to the heavy stumps gave way. I woke to the sound of a crash and a constant rushing, like the rumble of a waterfall hurtling beneath us. I nudged Case awake.

"Hey there. Hey, babe. Case? Can you hear something?"

"What? No."

"Really? I think it's probably a burst pipe, or maybe trouble at the tanks. But it could be something serious."

"Well, go see then."

"We both need to get up, babe."

"No… really?"

"Yes. Can't you hear that?" I stretched my arms and sat up. The noise was much louder now.

"Look, this might sound crazy, but does it feel like we're moving to you? Unless it's the booze?"

Within a few seconds I felt a violent jarring, followed by a loud bang. A head of water had crashed into the hut. I ran to the window. Bauxite mud was flooding into a collapsed underground system. In an arterial rush, some distant heart deep within the earth was summoning back its life force. Our building had skidded from its concrete base and was barreling into a gully, carried by the tremendous current.

"Shit! What the hell? Get up. Everyone!" I shouted. The hut crashed about and swayed in the narrow gulf of muddy rapids. I could not keep my balance so I sat on the bed. The walls banged and rattled, the roof creaked and strained above the rush of the sweeping tide. Our billet had become a makeshift raft. As the crew woke, pandemonium broke out. I could hear the others shouting now. My heart was racing. We had entered another wide channel and were careening down it at full tilt. I clamped my hands onto the bedstead. The angle was sixty or more degrees – all of our things tumbled into heaps and piled up in corners. Light glinted off the moving current. "Jesus – we're dipping and sliding on a river of mud. Case! For Christ's sake hold on to me!"

She drew herself up beside me. "I'm here. We've got this!"

We looked out again and were both stone amazed. I sat there praying that it wasn't happening.

Upstream, a fissure had opened on the mount. Everything was tumbling into it.

"I can't see over the gully banks from the window. How the fuck are we going to get out of here?"

"The whole mountain's come alive," Case said. Then she uttered several, 'Fucks', and looked for more clothes. I couldn't say anything more. I reached out and pulled on my jeans. Was it a nightmare? Was I actually awake? I shouted to Mike and Mo. "Can you feel this, guys? Get up! Mo, for God's sake look out. See where we are!"

Another tremendous wrenching sound; the crunch of splitting timbers. I watched the ceiling above Mike's flop tear across the main joinery; as we dipped sharply, it split around the bathroom. The night lights went out and the whole place lurched and bumped again. At the opposite end, the rafters gave more quickly. We suddenly felt Mo's end of the hut jolt downwards, then drop away into the torrent. The whole end had sheared off from ours. Everything beyond the bathroom was gone in an instant. I saw Mo's and Juanita's berth spin into a writhing current and skewer onto a broken pylon, jammed against the right bank. They never called out. I lost sight of them and their berth shortly afterwards. Tossing about in the current, some of our furniture bobbed and weaved about until it was dashed against the side of the gully. The stream continued to take us further down the slope. As we dressed and tried to come to terms with what to do next, the long cabin righted itself. Mud began to seep over the open end.

"Jesus, Clark, I can't… I just don't believe what's happened. They both just barreled into the bank. Are they…?"

"They both gone, Case," shouted Mike. "We gonna sink. Let's get out!"

"How? All I can see is racing mud and water. Look up on the mount. I think the new seams are gone. Swept away." We both climbed back onto the bed. The open end of the hut had tilted up.

"Maybe the lake's burst?" said Anne.

"I tink a cave system fell in," Mike shouted. The rush of the water was deafening now. I could just about hear Mike above the roar. "We gotta get off, Clark. Lots of huts behind us. We not de only ones. Maybe they gonna hit us. What we gonna do?" Following us downstream were other huts, broken loose on the swell.

"Is Case all right? I can't hear her," shouted Anne. I was frozen for a moment, unable to think, move or do anything useful. I tried to pull myself together.

"She's fine. She's here next to me. Can you guys get over to us?"

The floor began sloping towards the torrent. I held onto the bed. Water and mud swept in, splashing our end. At that, we were flung violently downwards again. This time Case was thrown against the bed posts. She screamed as she banged her elbows. A sudden surge of rocks hit our corner outside and the wardrobes tipped over on us. All our things spilled out across the floor. I pushed the cupboard sideways and checked to see if Case was alright. Clothes disappeared down the walkway and into the torrent. The noise was terrific. A horrid grinding of metal sounded above the hurtling rush of mud and water.

"Our half is still moving," I said "I think we are mid-flow. Stay on the beds. They're solid enough to take it. We might be able to ride it out." Mike was shouting for me again. "No, we gotta get out Clark!"

"I can't hear you, Mike?" I called back.

Finally, he screamed at me, "Coming over. Bathroom's splintered, our end's floodin'. All our stuff, tables, chairs — everything's gone."

"All right, all right. Get over here."

I heard them shouting, grabbing, slipping on the wet floor. Anne screamed as she banged her knees on the divider. "A rock! A big rock has wedged against the bed. Christ! We need to get out now, Clark. Help us get out. Please! Case, where are you?" Anne had flown into an almighty panic.

Case found her voice and yelled for Anne to get over quickly. I stood upright, struggling to see through the end window.

"Anne, climb the divider."

"For fuck's sake, Clark! We're heading over the ridge!" she yelled.

"Doesn't look like it, believe me," I yelled back. "We've swung left and downwards. The hut's tumbling into a sort of fissure that's opened. It's pretty steep, but maybe we'll get stuck."

Mud was pushing up through the floorboards now. Case leaned down off the bed and began to snatch up our photographs and letters. Helping her pick out the floating packages, I caught hold of a book of my notes and her sister's letters, washed into a corner. She grabbed my journal, my certificates and some more of my notebooks. We piled them on the bed. I managed to grab a handful of belts, clothes and accessories. She reached out for her jewellery box and tied it together. As the hut pitched again, our cameras and backpacks skidded off tables and shot towards the open end. Mike had scrambled up onto the divider now. He was holding onto Anne.

"Shit, we're losing everything!"

"Us too. But we'll make it!" Case put out a hand to Mike and we helped him over to our side. I climbed up and hoisted Anne onto the wide ledge. She swung her feet over herself, jumped down and landed on our muddied bed.

"Are we going to live through it?" asked Anne. I looked at Mike.

"We've lost our things, but we're not losing each other," I said.

"We've already lost Mo and Juanita. I think they're dead!" Anne turned and fell into Mike's arms.

"You don't know that for sure, Anne. They may be lodged in the gully. We just don't know."

The remains of the hut lurched as our combined weight changed the balance. A heavy current swept across the floor, taking the rest of our precious memories — and most of our lives until now — with it. We clung on tightly to anything that felt the least bit solid. It was too late to grab anything more. The flow exited through the front entrance, smashing the front door off its hinges. Water surged across the open floor and pooled into the corner as we tilted. We levelled up a bit and the water ran off, leaving a thick, malodorous sludge behind. I paced my breathing. The four of us were huddled together on the bed. Case stared staring blindly at the gaping hole where the door had been.

"Any ideas about how to get off this fucking thing?" she yelled.

"We've slowed, but all I can see is rocky walls either side of us. There's nothing to climb out onto."

Anne buried her face in the bedclothes. Case gently rubbed her shoulders.

"Let's get onto the roof, Clark. Maybe it's high enough to jump to the bank?"

"Agreed. Let's try it." As I thought about that suggestion, I looked at Mike. Our eyes locked. We'd both felt us rise a notch, pivoting on the rear edge. "I think we've hit a stem in the flow." I said. "The increased pressure is pushing us upwards. For God's sake, everyone hang on."

The fissure wasn't far off now. We'd travelled about a hundred metres along the gully.

"No!" cried Mike. He grabbed Case and they rushed to the opposite side of our room to try and balance us out. I saw him put his back to the wall and push with all his might.

"It's no good," I said. "Get the fuck back here! It'll never work."

We were rising at an alarming rate now. The beds began to lift from the floor. Case and Mike gave up and ran back to us, shaking their heads. "Oh, Jesus, I thought we were out of it," said Case.

Mike whispered something to Anne softly and she seemed to buck up a little. I tore the bed sheets off and wrapped the remains of our things in the centre. Mike tied the bundle to the ceiling joist. We were still rising slowly, up and up, degree by degree, the rear edge grinding on the base rock as we tipped. The force of the water was building all the time, pressing against the underside.

"We've got to climb out!" Case said, looking up at the open doorway above us. The door was completely gone. Jets of water started to pour in through the splits in the floor as we tipped further over. As the floor became the wall in front of us, we leaned against the back wall, angled toward the mattress. I stood up, straddling our wall posters, praying we didn't tip right over. The old roof would never take the pressure.

There was a crash near the exit. We turned our heads simultaneously. A heavy, wet rope dangled over the near-vertical floor. I edged along the bed and looked up into the gap. The rope had been shot from the bank.

"We've got to give it a try."

"It's a bloody miracle shot!" I said. "Case, hold my waist." I grabbed hold of the rope. A spray of water was jetting right at me now, striking me full in the chest. The floor was buckling too. It wouldn't be long. "This whole place is coming apart. Case, you first." I tied the rope around her waist, then tugged hard on it. Case climbed her way up past the floor and reached out of the door frame. She put her hands on either side and heaved herself through the opening. Thank God she was out.

Anne leapt up and shouted, "Hurry, Case, get us out of here. You can do it!"

"One's climbed out, Hal. She's on the side. See? Get over there, man." The voices from the bank were lost to us in the noise and the dust.

"There's four of us." I heard case Case shout. "Clark, I'm signaling the bank. They've fired ropes across the gully. It's a haze of dirt and searchlights up here. But I think a line's been rigged across the gulley. I can hardly breathe with all the dirt in the air."

"Hold on!" a man yelled from the bank. "We sending a man out!" he shouted again but I couldn't hear anything more above the thrashing torrent.

"Case, throw the rope down so we can join you!"

A searchlight beam outlined Case's figure in the doorway among the dust and debris. Long shadows shimmered over the cabin. Flashes came in through the windows and beams of light broke though the splits in the floor. You could smell the musky heaviness of earth and mud. A loud bang came from the bank. Another line reached us. Case caught hold of it and pushed the rope through the doorway into the hut.

"C'mon! Anne, get up here! Move."

I could barely see the line as it dropped down. The floorboards had separated now and muddy water was still gushing across my chest, cold and heavy. I shivered, tired; tired of pushing back against the fountaining water. I struggled to fasten the rope to Anne. Mike got under her and we heaved her upwards between us. All three of us were dripping wet. I heard loud cannon fire coming from the bank. We guessed it was more lines being shot out.

I shouted up to Case. She grabbed Anne's hand from above.

"Hold on, honey. Pull yourself up."

Mike gave a last shove under Anne's hips and finally she managed pull herself through the gap. Once free, she gasped for breath. Case ripped off a portion of her shirt and placed it across Anne's mouth." Here, it will help. The air tastes poisoned."

I looked up, trying to guess where they were and what was going on out there.

"Case? Throw the line in." The open doorway was three metres above us.

"I'm throwing the line back in," Case shouted. She'd not heard me. As she began untying Anne, she drew her away from the opening.

"Clark. We've got to get you both out. You'll see – there's more chance out here."
A rope fell across my face. I caught hold of it. The hut had stopped rising but it juddered frequently with the force of the current. I thought it had reached its death throes.

"This is it, Mike. Get out. You first. I'm light enough to try it without a rope."

"All right, fix me the line," he said.

I made a couple of knots along the rope's length, then looped the end around Mike's waist. I dodged the worst of the stream and tapped his arm. "Go!" He pulled hard, heaving himself up to the first knot. He groaned horribly as he climbed. The rope smacked against the side of the hut as it tightened. He gave another loud groan, going hand over hand as he hauled himself up towards the gap. I pushed him hard from underneath, steadying his feet as they swung above me.

The water was at my waist level now. Mike had lifted his knees up and was dragging himself outside. I felt again for the side wall, shivering badly now. The pain of being literally freezing cold is different to a fun day on a sledge in the snow. But while bracing myself, the wall folded inwards. A long splinter pierced the top of my thigh and I saw it come out the other side. I couldn't stop myself from screaming. Case banged on the wall near the opening.
"What the hell's going on, Clark?"
I tried to move. No use. I began to hyperventilate, shuddering from the pain. I couldn't think straight, I was shaking so badly. I looked down at the wound: a long white splinter poking up through the thigh muscle. The tip had scraps of material stuck to it. I cleared the bloody water away from the wound, but it was hard to see how bad it was. I knew I was pinned. What the hell could I do? I was going into shock. Christ was this it? Really?

Drowned in a smashed hut on a tide of mud and rocks? But I'd lived no life at all!

The water, relentless now, was pouring through every crack, mud oozing into the big split beside me, filling the angle between the floor and wall of the hut. I began to panic. I banged my fists on the rear wall. Anne yelled down at me in the darkness.

"What's happened, Clark?"

I tried to speak but my tongue went rigid in my mouth. Case was outside, yelling for help. I grabbed hold of the bed and squeezed the posts hard, trying to subdue the pain as best I could. The splinter was still attached to the board in the wall. I was going to have to snap it free. As the water was rising, I took a breath, twisted my hips violently, then gasped. The splinter held firm.

"Shit, shit, shit!" I felt the muscle tear. I'd made the wound worse. I cried out, "Mike, I'm pinned. A splinter, need to jerk it free." I had to try again. One last time. After a deep breath I yelled loudly as I twisted away from the wall. This time it worked. My hair stood on end as the long sliver of wood tore free from the muscle. Blood clouded the muddy water. Two boards suddenly snapped backwards, and I saw a section of the hut disappear with the long splinter. This new hole in the side wall started letting the water out. Christ, at least I was saved from drowning. As the hut drained, blood ran freely down my legs. It pooled around my ankles in the water. I rubbed my eyes. Hard to see now – getting darker. I felt giddy, like I was going to pass out. Slowly I managed to tear a strip off my shirt and tie it tightly around my thigh to stem the bleeding. I knew I'd lost way too much blood. Mike was leaning halfway in, looking toward the open end. I guess he was trying to see if I'd been swept away. A search lamp reflected off his body and bounced light into the cabin. I spoke feebly. "I'm here, Mike. Below you."

"Jesus! Man, you bleedin' bad. Am coming in."

"No, big man. Drop down the rope. I'm coming out. Haul me up. I can't use my left leg."

A beam of light entered the gap and showed up the thick haze of dust and debris falling through the air. I started coughing.

The line went taut as Mike hauled me off the floor. With the weight off my leg, it felt strangely better. My head was spinning. I swallowed hard. God, I needed a drink. I felt so damn tired. Several pairs of hands grabbed at me as my head poked through the opening. I looked straight at Case. She grabbed my shoulders and with Mike's help, dragged me away from the gap.

Anne was kneeling by me. "Thank God, Clark. Come here, darling. What the hell happened?" She started wiping the blood from my face and hands.

"I'm okay. Got pinned by a splintered board." My eyes were stinging in the haze. I coughed hard. I could see Case half clinging to a shot line rigged across the torrent. The main line was a good inch in diameter. It looked like it would hold. A thinner pull line had been wrapped around a makeshift loop. I guessed the whole rig was a kind of emergency zip wire.

I stared at Anne — she looked all in. Mike hunkered down next to me, exhausted too. "There's nothing else survived this far down. It looks like we're it. The other huts are gone. Jeez! You could lose a few pouns, Clark."

I smiled, "Thanks, big man. That your rig on the line?"

"This part. But they're coming over with a chair. Too dangerous to juss hook over."

A bosun's chair was being rigged across the gully. The staging was already well fixed on each bank. CATs and dozers on opposite sides were keeping the main line taut.

The whole place was flooded with a misty light, engines roaring, Jennys going full blast. I shaded my eyes again from the dust cloud and the lights.

"What about Mo? Juanita? Anything? Can you see them?"

"In this?" coughed Anne.

"No, Clark," whispered Mike. "They gone. No good looking now."

Anne was shaking her head. She spoke tearfully. "A couple of hours ago, we were dancing. It was just perfect. How could this have happened? How can they both be dead?"

To rig the chair, a crewman arrived on a death slide looped over the line. He'd fought the steep angle pretty well. I was damned glad to see him! The heavily muscled Negro wore coveralls and a breather mask. He landed square onto us, steadied himself then sloughed off the heavy coil of rope he'd slung across his body. He was even bigger than Mike. Case got up and helped him unpack the seat planks. As they tied the knots through the holes in the wood, Mike helped fix the gant line. The crewman clipped a nylon safety harness to the main line above us.
"I think they gonna shoot a safety across. Don't know when – but should be soon anyhow."

Mike helped Anne onto the stay first. "Just like a ski-lift, ma'am," the crewman said, calmly. "Sit comfortable now. We gonna get you all off safe." Anne was holding back her tears. "Don't worry none." The crewman whirled his hand above his head, flashing a torchlight. Slowly Anne began her journey. The steep edges of the fissure had kept the torrent barrelling one way. The angle of the subsided hut meant Anne had to walk uphill before stepping off into the darkness. She looked down at the tall wave that was breaking against the floor of the hut, pressing hard and fast.

"Eyes tight shut now, miss," the crewman said.

Further downstream, the flow was still disappearing into the chasm. The ruined building lurched under us. I instinctively grabbed at the slack shot line. The back wall juddered again. I held onto Mike and we grabbed for Case together. The half building twisted awkwardly in the current. We struggled to keep our balance. "It's trying to turn itself out of the flow," I said. "Underneath, the floor wood's giving way." I sat down and crawled up to the edge. In the torrent below us, ripped-up trees, roofing and a car door swept past me into the darkness. I glanced over my shoulder. Mike was busy watching Anne being hauled to safety.

"You're next, Case!" I shouted. Debris continued to rain down.

"No, you're bleeding, Clark. You need to go next. Not me."

Mike looked at my wound. "You gotta get that looked at. God, some split. How ya feel?"

"It's not so bad now. I've stopped the worst of the bleeding."

Case drew closer. "You don't look so good to me. You're pale and cold. Maybe you should loosen that tourniquet?"

"Its fine – another few minutes maybe."

"Please go next. You're shaking. Is it the pain?"

"Probably."

"You've lost a lot of blood."

"If you're handling it, Case, I'll be fine. You know, are you ever afraid of anything?"

"Yes — I've always been afraid of rough seas crashing on a beach."

"Drowning is—"

"Not drowning, or currents. Riptides they call them, don't they?

"Yes."

"But why are you so afraid of riptides?"

"Because I saw myself in a dream, dead on a beach, washed ashore, tangled in netting and weed; crabs and starfish crawling over me." I saw she looked gaunt and fearful in the misty light.

"Well, that's not going to happen here. We're on a roof – not a beach."

"They're hauling the chair back, Clark, just go for God's sake." She pleaded with me again, but I took no notice.

"You're next, babe." I called out. "That right, Mike?" The crewman stepped over us.

"Ladies first," he said. "Be just a minute now."

It was too dark to see exactly where Anne had landed, but a torch signaled she'd got across safely.

"When did all this begin?" Mike asked the crewman.

"Oh, 'bout an hour ago. We got straight on it. Soon as de gulf opened, the centre of camp was gone in a flash, but de lower terrace had several CATs parked up. And de last crew were still washing down. They had dozers in ready for tomorrow on the upper ridge. Mighty lucky, they on de other side of dat gully."

"And the ore – the tanks?" Mike asked.

"Ain't no more mine — all slipped back into de earth."

The empty chair reached us. Case stood up carefully as it clattered over the roof. I flopped over onto my back and stared into the dust cloud. I felt dizzy and cold. Thick mud lay on my wet shirt. The remaining walls we were relying on tremored again as large rocks and branches crashed against the floor below. I knew we had to get Case off. I wiped my hands on my shirt, my palms all sticky with blood and mud.

"Take care!" I squinted to see her in the mix of stark light and darkness.

"Okay." She climbed onto the stay and put the safety harness on.

"Hang on tight." I blew a kiss to her.

"I'll be fine." The crewman gave his signal and Case walked slowly off the edge of the hut, ready to swing out over the torrent. The crewman shouted. "It best wid eyes closed, darlin'."

Mike stepped over me. Then he lay down too and held on to the slackened shot line. I knew what he was going to say.

"You next, Clark."

"No, you. We may not have long."

"Look, I know Anne's safe. I be there soon enough. Join Case, fo' me."

I gritted my teeth. "All right." I heard Case shout and looked out across the gully. The haze was very thick, but I could see her white shirt swaying in the light. "You okay, Case?" I yelled. I listened hard but heard no reply. The crewman shone his torch into the dark. I caught sight of the line wavering above us. The hut shook again. Part of the roof had lifted away from the trusses. As the rear wall sagged, the crewman slipped and fell. Mike shot out an arm and grabbed his leg. They both held on. Mike helped him climb to his feet.

"I'm okay. Thanks. Now, when de chair's back, who's goin?" We said nothing. "Okay, you bleedin'. Yo goin' next." He pointed to me. I had no idea how long the hut would stay wedged in this position. Half the roof was way downstream now. I could hear it smashing into the banks as it broke up.

"Can the line hold us both?" The crewman looked right at me, fixing me with a cold gaze. He looked very concerned. "Mebbe – but it risky," he said. "Least, it ain't rigged for two heavies." Then he made his decision. "Mike, yo go first. Then maybe we go together. Me an' him. He's a skinny one." He nodded to me. The chair clattered back onto the side of the hut.

Our beds suddenly crashed through the broken walls into the torrent. I saw the mattresses separate and tumble down stream. They vanished from sight in the blink of an eye. We pulled the chair further in and I helped get Mike ready. He pushed me away. "I'm okay. You sit down." Hobbling back from the edge, I sat down out of breath, coughing hard. The pain was hot — searing hot — in my thigh. Pains grated across my spine.

"Chair lines be all twisted! Gotta be put right." The crewman was wrestling with the knots. He untied the seat then retied the gant line. Mike got to the seat and sat down on the plank.

"Harness missin'. Must have fallen off in de water – p'raps they forget to fix it in de rush?"

"Just go. Fo'get it," Mike said, I peered at him from slanted eyes. The hut rocked, dropping lower as he walked.

"God! We're sinking, Mike. Not long now."

"I'm prayin', Clark, but we gonna get you off too. Stay calm." Mike looked over the edge. I lay out flat again, keeping my leg bent a little. It hurt too much to straighten it. The dust kept coming down, caught in the sweeping lamps that threw bright yellow arcs across our faces. "Loosen that tourney now, Clark. They need a loosen now an' again. I read about tourneys."

"Alright. I won't forget. See you."

The crewman held the gant stays firmly until Mike reached the edge.

"Let the line take the weight. At the edge, lean out easy."

He watched the big man lean forward. Mike stepped off and the rope jumped tight as it took his weight. Spatters of mud and water sprinkled the hut as the haul line took up the strain. I watched him swing downwards. Dust swirled around him. The wind had picked up now and the lights on the banks flickered on and off. Distant lightning flashed in the sky, followed by a long peal of thunder. Mike continued along in a rising storm of earth, twigs and leaves. The line above us twanged and shook. Halfway across, Mike disappeared into the night. I waited for the lamps to find him and light his bulk. The crewman attached a rope to the slack shot line.

I turned to see our white bundle of things hanging on an exposed joist inside. I got the man's attention. "Hey, can you reach that?" I pointed to the bundle.

"Maybe," he said slowly. Most of the roof had broken away. To me it looked an easy climb in.

"What's your name, man? I don't even know your name," I shouted.

"Hal," he said.

"Okay, Hal. That's our precious things. They mean a big deal to us, man. Can you reach them? I'll hold onto you." He swung down and crawled along the beam. Moving to a parallel rafter, I watched him untie the bundle. He cast it over his shoulder and edged his way back to me. "Here, you take it now." He threw the bag hard. I just caught it. There was a sudden crack and I heard the shot line go taut and slap against the wood repeatedly, as if kicking itself. Then the main line snapped violently. I left our bundle of things and squinted into the night: nothing. I looked for Mike. The lights had dimmed on the banks. A lone beam scanned the air. I could hear a commotion on the bank above the rushing of the water. Hal had pulled himself out of the doorframe and was climbing up beside me.

"Whass goin on?" he said breathlessly.

"I don't know. Where's the line? Where's Mike? Mike!" I called out again, but there was no reply."

"Line gone," said Hal, gripping my arm. I could see he was afraid.

"What? It can't have. Have they hauled it in? Maybe it's twisted again."

"Line always been high and straight. It gone."

We searched the darkness. Hal waved his torch, scoping the narrow beam across the gully. I felt dizzy and numb, sick with worry and short of breath. I couldn't feel my leg at all now. I shouted for Mike again with all the breath I had left. There was no reply. Jesus, no, not the big man. How could that happen? The crewman saw my distress and took off his face mask.

"Here, put this on . . . breathe easy now." He helped me pull the air filter over my mouth.

"I never heard a thing." I gasped. "No screams or shouts. Where is he? What the hell happened to him?"

"I think he just gone. Lord save his soul."

We looked down into the flow. Flares were being fired; red rockets scorched the night sky. They lit the dust and their red glow intensified the ruby muds that had taken Mike from us. There was no sign of the big man below. The back edge of the hut thrashed against the bedrock as I lay on my belly searching the gully. The speed of the current was so fierce. I'd never seen that much water, mud and rock. I edged back. Breathing easier, I grabbed the slack shot line again.

"Signal back." I told him. "Now!" I pulled my bundle over the shot line. Hal swirled his torch above his head. The storm was getting closer. Rain was pitting the dust on the wall of the hut now. Lights flashed up again from the bank. We heard shouts. Hal tugged three times on the shot line and it began to move up into the air, while I separated a sheet from the bundle and doubled it over the line. I made a sling to put my good leg through. We needed to keep our heads; if so, there was a chance we'd make it. Hal grabbed his loop rope and slung it over again. I saw the CAT on the opposite side lower its arm so we could slide back faster. The angle looked nearly a third steeper to me. The rain shone white as it caught in the searchlights. We began to edge ourselves out along the line, swinging our legs to get forward motion. My torn leg dangled beneath me in the dark.

"Hang on, Hal." I had to stop. "My leg feels numb. Can't feel a thing." I reached down and loosened the tourniquet. We waited a minute, both of us sitting in mid-air, not daring to look down, breathing as shallowly as we could. More shouts came from the bank.

"We muss go now, Clark."

There was a tearing of wood and metal. I heard the bathroom sinks crash to the floor. The dorm walls buckled inwards. The last of the hut finally imploded in on itself, as if crushed by an invisible, giant fist; glass shattered into the night and the roof tore into shreds. Hal grabbed at my waist. There was a cannon shot from the bank. I heard a new line come whistling at us.

"Fuck! I can't see it. Which side is it?" I cried out. Hal had kept one foot on the corner of what was left of the hut. Suddenly, the ball of caved remains took a half turn and spun away from us. The edge whipped from under him as he lurched over. I watched our former abode hurtle off downstream, its mangled form bumping and groaning as it went. We were left suspended on the thinner shot line. I dared not move or breathe. Would it hold both of us?

"Jeez, I got it, man!" he said. "I fuckin' caught it."

"I can't believe it, Hal. Thank God!"

He'd snatched the haul line from the air as it sailed past us. I put an arm up as he looped it around my shoulders and chest. Across the chasm, the crews began to inch us to safety.

It might have taken hours. I don't remember clearly. That crawling journey only ended when my feet finally touched solid ground. I was shaking too much to stand. I could barely balance. The pain in my leg mixed with the joy of survival – I didn't know whether to laugh or cry. From nowhere, Case suddenly rushed up to me as I was being unhitched.

"Thank fuck!" She buried her head into my neck and clung onto me. I felt her nails dig into my ribs and I felt her tears on my face.

"I think some of our stuff fell out on the way over," I said swinging the little bundle I'd kept into her hands. She moved away from to peek inside.

"Come here, you bastard!" She flung herself at me again. I hugged her tight. My legs gave way. We fell to earth together, my teeth chattering against her shoulder.

Anne was nowhere to be seen. "Anne?"

"Already on her way to hospital." Case burst into tears again, but recovered quickly and smiled at me, wiping her eyes and face. Forcing a smile, she said, "It's all going to be all right – isn't it? Your leg will heal. We will move on.

I tried to smile. We were both sniveling wrecks. I looked round for Hal. He was sitting with his head in his hands a little way off. Case helped me crawl over to him. She held him close. "Thank you – thank you so much," she said and she kissed him — simply, quietly. He touched her face. Then he looked long at her with those coal-black eyes of his that had earlier fixed on me so gravely.

"You most welcome, miss," he said. I bent and squeezed Hal's arm.

"Thank God you caught the line! We *are* okay? Aren't we?"

"Sho' ting, boss. I'm sorry about – about ..."

"It's okay, Hal. The big man's gone. It was not your fault. Many friends died tonight. And God, I'm sorry for that."

Case straightened up to her full height and pointed out a site foreman running towards us in a white hat. Medics were also on their way. He stopped abruptly, almost comically, on the hill. He called for blankets, then waved them down towards us. Eventually he arrived, breathless, and looked at us slowly, marveling from head to toe.

"My God – you both survived!" he said, clearly shocked. "The only people from that quadrant. That rescue seemed impossible. We've lost half the camp tonight. The workings are gone. Where is the man who went across?"

I pointed to Hal. The official nodded. Another man came up and handed me a blanket, turned and gently wrapped Case in one. "Good lord, you're in a bad way, lad, aren't you? Let's get you both off to hospital."

I smiled at his pressed shirt and linen trousers, only slightly dusty. The red clouds were thinning now and the rain was coming down harder. I pulled off my dust mask. At last the torrent had slowed, its hellbent rush quietened. I wondered how much of the mine went into the sea . . . and maybe Mike had managed to . . . I pulled my blanket up around my shoulders and shivered.

Managing to hobble uphill together, we inched ahead arm in arm, Case and me, with our white, bedraggled bundle of belongings, up past the new loaders that had arrived from Alumina Holdings then towards where the road to the canteen had been. I slowed at the junction.

"Fuck, can you believe it? Look! It's all gone, everything," I said. "Swallowed by the mountain."

Where our lives had been lived there was nothing now but blackness and cold rain.

"Our pool might still be there," she said. I cuddled her close. Right now, we couldn't look any further. Two men carrying a stretcher arrived. They lifted me up. Case smiled.

"On ya get, soldier!"

I swung my leg up and fell into the stretcher. They moved quickly. The ambulance was further up the hill among the lights. She saw me grinning. "You and your bed!"

When we got to the vehicle, Case climbed in tiredly. They slid me onto a side bench. A guy outside slammed the door, banged his fist twice on the side and we were whisked away. The siren blared into the night.

After a moment, I whispered, "I'm worried about Anne."

Case looked at me teary-eyed. "She saw him drop, Clark. Went all to pieces. They've taken her to hospital. I don't know where. I'll try and get hold of the roster when we get to Port Maria. I really can't believe it. Mike just vanished."

That was something no-one could ever understand. Who chooses who lives and dies – fate? God? luck? In the suddenness lies disbelief. Our survival still hadn't sunk in. We were supposed to feel, lucky – brave even . . . All I felt was tired and crushed.

Case kept repeating the words. 'One moment Mike was there, the next gone.' She told me what had happened on the opposite bank, while I was searching the torrent from the roof.

"They tried throwing a couple of buoys with lines attached. They even cut the lights and looked with a beam. I asked for flares. Krebbs fired a first - it soared up and out over the torrent, a single red star in the night. He fired two more. We waited as the rockets dropped slowly from the sky; but there was nothing. No sign of anyone. Ten minutes had passed – nothing. Men were sent to look further downstream for him. But nothing's been reported."

"God help him, and her," I said. I reached out to Case. She stroked my face.

"I suppose we just thank God we're out of it."

"I need to go to Mo's mother. Up to Dale Case. I don't know when, but I have to go."

"You want to go back there, after all that's happened?"

"I have to. How couldn't I?"

"She'll think you're gloating about survival. Surely you don't mean to go? It might be dangerous. She warned you – and Mo. Think it over, darling. Let it rest, until you're better."

"Mo's dead. It's not gloating - it's respect. I need to face her, if she'll see me."

"Then I should go with you."

"No, I'll go alone. I owe her that much."

"I never thought it would end this way, Clark. What we had was so beautiful."

I pointed to the bundle she was carrying. "Open it. Hal and Mike rescued our stuff."
It brightened her to untie the torn, stained sheets.

"Not sure everything's there," I warned. "Might have dropped things."

I could see the jewellery box had gone. I waited for her rebuke. None came. It felt good to be let off.

A medic began examining my leg again. He unwound the filthy bandage and whistled. "Phew! You lucky – very lucky. You don' pierce de femoral artery."

Case bit her lips as she picked through our things. Nixie's letters were smeared red.

Epilogue

Five days later we were sitting in a junior suite at the Bristol. DALCO had paid us half what we were owed. More payments were promised after the inquests. The funerals had started — they would stretch through the rest of the month. Many were undertaken with empty caskets. The brass names stood engraved on small plaques. Mike, Juanita's and Mo's were this Friday. Case had shopped yesterday and a new charcoal jacket was hanging in the wardrobe for me. There were bags of new clothes still littering the floor; nearly all of them replacements. We had been given a small amount of cash and a suite for three weeks. Was it enough – for what we had been through? It was hard to put a price on lives that had changed overnight. What price is a life worth?

Case came over to the bed. I was still hobbling because of the muscle tear. Estimates of six to eight weeks were run by me at the outpatients' clinic, where twice a week Case took me to have my dressings changed. Clambering into a taxi and sitting for an hour in a bleak, busy room did little to stop the flashbacks . . . Back at the Bristol I was content to sleep off the meds. Case tenderly put a small parcel on the pillow next to me. I opened my eyes to look at it.

"When you're ready. It'll keep," she said quietly. I wanted to sit up.

"What is it?"

"Something that was tucked into the bundle you handed me."

It looked to me like Mo's writing. There was no cover and the pages were all stained pink. I picked up a sheet and read. It was still damp in the centre.

'I basked early that morning in the rain-freshened acres of Sweet Briar Farm. For many years its fields had lain fallow. Today I'd come to watch sun-up, walk the dry furrows and kick sharp stones to the field edge. Grandfather had already ploughed here last week. When I'd looked too haughtily at the proceedings and stared into the hot sun with a smile, he'd told me to visit Edward's field before I went home.

'I walked across Mary Down and to my surprise, I was met by a field of swaying corn, circling on eddies in the wind. I loved watching the crops move — rippling and swirling like crowds on big race days. Despite the dry spell, this was a beautiful crop – strong and tall. I stopped and sat among the ripening corn; before the reaping, the gleaner looks on in doleful airs.

'I smelled the healthy green shoots; the cobs green with patches of yellow showing, some of the heads still encased in their leafy, fibrous cocoons. A reaching sky spun silken clouds . . .'

Mo's page of text ended abruptly here. I leaned over and opened the bedside drawer beside me. Looking into a little pouch of belongings I always carried with me now – a tiger's eye for inspiration, a quote from Gifford's Baviad for torment, and a strip of chokecherry bark to remind me of my past. I pulled out a scrawled note; a prose poem I'd abandoned. To go back to it today seemed suddenly apt. But strangely I was drawn back to reading more of Mo's pages. I never knew he kept jottings or a diary of sorts. I leafed through some damp entries and what I found surprised me. Between the sheets was the remnants of a scribble I'd discarded months ago. Mo must have rescued it. I read it out to Case …

'*At times, we feel the ghosts of our former selves inside us. They wait impatiently, brimming with energy, until a tiny trigger is pulled — like an old photograph or a whispered memory.*

How striking our face was back then, how wistful and magnificent it was when we rode on days of hedonism and dreams. Poor ghosts that followed those dreams; forlorn spirits that burned the hours in deeds long-forgotten – fickle mouths that laughed with dreary, faceless people. They return now – wreathed in smiles, laughing at who we became.

Drunk on words from days won in sunshine, our carefree selves return to form our worst regrets. It is getting late now. In the things we leave unspoken, in the things we leave undone, are the things that make our own undoing.

We might look closer in the hope of magnifying the light that remains within us — only to find that we can never be exactly how we seem.'

www.ingramcontent.com/pod-product-compliance
Lightning Source LLC
Chambersburg PA
CBHW060934050726
47592CB00003B/946